THE JACK REACHER CASES
CASES

THE MAN WHO WORKS ALONE

DAN AMES

A USA TODAY BESTSELLING BOOK

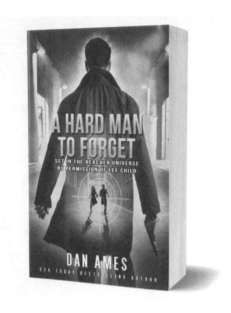

Book One in The JACK REACHER Cases

THE JACK REACHER CASES

The Man Who Works Alone

by

Dan Ames

No one was cheered and nothing was discussed;
Column by column in a cloud of dust

-W.H. Auden

CHAPTER 1

HE WAS no stranger to the sight of blood.

Nor was the image of such a tremendous amount of blood foreign to him.

No, what troubled him at the moment was that the blood was his.

The man known only as Paco dragged his battered body across the hotel room floor and struggled to grasp his bloody cell phone. His hands shook and he cursed himself for not being better prepared.

Ever since he'd left active service and become a private soldier for hire – a mercenary – he'd always worked alone. It wasn't that he hadn't enjoyed the camaraderie of his fellow special ops soldiers. In fact, he was still good friends with many of them. His decision to be a lone wolf, to be a man who worked alone had to do with his desire for operational control. He'd grown to hate the decision-making process of a larger military unit and since then had relished being the entire control and command apparatus for each mission.

Until now.

Which is why, as he felt the blood gush from his wounds, he knew there was no point in finding blame elsewhere.

It had been his mission. His decisions.

Impeccable planning was one of his hallmarks and this mission had not been up to his usual standards. For that, he avoided the temptation to fault the accelerated schedule and abbreviated timeline – two factors he had overlooked because of the oversized paycheck – instead he took full responsibility for his current predicament.

Still it pissed him off.

He finally managed to grasp the cell phone and he went directly to his contacts. The first person he wanted to call was probably the best fit for what he needed. Plus, he didn't live far from Vegas and could be here in time to possibly save his life.

He had blood on his hands and the phone was slippery between his fingers.

Paco heard footsteps outside the door.

Of course they followed me, he thought. *No surprise there.*

For a moment, he hesitated. He was down to his last gun and by his own count only had a few rounds left. The running gun battle had been an obscene display of firepower. Paco still couldn't believe the cops hadn't intervened. Hey, it was Vegas, he guessed. Anything can happen.

More blood seeped from his gunshot wounds. He wasn't sure how many times he'd been hit but he knew he'd taken rounds in the shoulder, stomach, leg and hip. He knew the hip wasn't bad as it had glanced off his bone instead of crashing into his pelvis. If that had happened he wouldn't have been able to walk let alone run.

The hip hurt like hell, which was odd because out of everything it was the stomach wound that would kill him. A gut shot was slow death, but it was usually death nonetheless.

Paco tapped on the contact's cell phone and then hit the speaker button. He placed the phone on the floor and picked up his last remaining gun, a .45. It felt surprisingly light and now he wasn't sure if he had any rounds left at all. He quickly ejected the magazine, saw he had three bullets left, plus one in the chamber, and then slammed it back home.

Four shots at life, he thought.

Paco heard the door to his hotel room beep and saw the green light momentarily flash. He was impressed once again. He couldn't believe they had found him so fast and now, they'd even managed to get a key to his room.

Whomever his opponents were, they were good.

Very good.

He glanced down at the phone and saw the call connect.

A voice told him to leave a message.

At the same time, the door swung open and Paco saw the empty hallway beyond and then it was instantly filled with the orange and red flash of gunfire as a shape moved in. Paco fired center mass but the bullet that entered his forehead made it to his brain first – before the knowledge he'd missed all of his shots arrived.

His last vision was the shape stepping into the room, smoke in front of his eyes and the room tilting sideways and fading to black.

The killer stood over Paco and fired another round into the man's skull.

He glanced down at the phone. It appeared the target had been in the process of leaving someone a message. The killer didn't know exactly how much information had been conveyed. He peered more closely at the phone and read the name of the contact the newly dead man had called. The killer then pointed his gun at the phone and fired a bullet into it. It shattered.

He didn't need the phone, anyway.

All he needed was the name, which he'd been able to read.

It was a name he didn't know.

Michael Tallon.

CHAPTER 2

ONE HOUR EARLIER

Mikael Gladhus, CEO of Gladcon, Inc., stared in drunken fascination at the female escort stripping off her clothes in front of him. She was utterly without inhibition and she was going much too fast.

"Wait," he said. She was a tall, lithe blonde. Mikael could see her dark roots and hoped that he wouldn't be able to compare anything natural down below. He preferred his hookers be completely shaved. Smooth as glass.

He hadn't intended to wind up here in a hotel in Vegas. It had just kind of happened. Normally a man of swift decisions, he'd gone back and forth on this one. Namely because it was the biggest one of his life.

He didn't know what to do frankly. He'd decided to move in one direction, driven by one emotion. And then, he'd had second thoughts, caused by an entirely different motivation.

Gladhus had almost pulled the trigger but then decided to hole up in a hotel room and think it through. Naturally, it being Las Vegas, he'd ordered the most expensive bottle of vodka from room service and then fortuitously crossed paths with this blonde beauty. He knew she was a professional – any woman who looked like this and lived in Vegas probably was.

Normally, when he was in town he got his girls from an outfit called Platinum Exports. He'd used them before many times here in Vegas and Los Angeles, too, and although their girls were the most expensive in town, in his opinion, they were also the best. Absolute top-notch quality.

She had unbuttoned her top, kicked off her stiletto heels and was in the process of sliding out of her black stockings. "Put your shoes back on," he said. His voice was slurred and his eyelids were at half-mast.

She hesitated and Mikael thought he may have

seen an eye roll. She did as she was told though and knelt down and strapped the heels back on.

Damn right you do what I tell you, if you want to make that money, he thought.

He watched as she fastened the straps of her heels. The move caused her ample breasts to squeeze together.

Mikael licked his lips in anticipation.

"Roll over," she said.

"What?"

"Roll over. I always start with a massage."

Her voice was clipped. Not American, he thought. Or maybe it was a fake accent to disguise the fact she was American. You never knew. This was a city of facades.

He liked how her tone carried a sense of command she was clearly used to.

He decided to play along and obey her.

The bed shifted slightly and Mikael felt her straddle him. He was already naked and quickly the sensation of warm oil being poured onto his back made him close his eyes. Her hands were already on him and soon, his muscles began to relax.

If she didn't tell him to flip over soon he was going to do it himself-

The sound of a click made him think the door

had just closed. But that was impossible. The girl was still on top of him.

He tried to turn but the girl slid up and pinned his arms in place with her knees. *She is stronger than she looks*, he thought.

Mikael felt her long nails scrape down his back. They pierced his skin and pain caused him to jerk upward but she pushed him back down. He tried to roll onto his back but she held him in position.

Something cold touched the back of his neck.

It was hard.

Metallic.

"What–"

"Shhh."

The CEO of Gladcon never felt the bullet that entered the base of his brain and left nothing in its wake but instant death.

He also didn't live to see the expensive hooker slip her clothes back on, gather his briefcase and laptop computer, and let herself out of the room.

CHAPTER 3

AH, *Vegas*.

Paco hadn't made a regular habit of coming to Sin City, but he was no stranger to it, either. Most guys like him who'd spent their entire lives in the military usually at one point or another touched down in Las Vegas.

Whether it was a meeting, convention or just to blow off steam, the city saw guys like Paco on a pretty regular basis.

But this trip was certainly not for pleasure.

Business had called in the form of a private contract submitted to Paco's business manager. That term was used loosely and sometimes sarcastically by Paco's fellow freelance soldiers.

In any event, the person who'd contacted Paco's go-between had done so via encrypted messaging and made him a lucrative offer: pick up a laptop and briefcase from another agent in Las Vegas and await further instructions on where and when to deliver them.

Easy enough.

Paco expressed no small amount of skepticism when he'd seen the sparse details of the job.

But the accompanying bid for Paco's service was quite high and he wondered why. He also wondered why there had been little time for planning and preparation. It was always like this in his line of work: the bigger the paycheck, the larger the risk.

Unfortunately, he'd had a mishap that required medical work and without insurance, he'd racked up a pretty hefty medical bill. This would cover it with plenty left over so he'd gone against his instincts and accepted the job.

Now, he sat in a busy coffee shop across from the entrance to the hotel from which the woman was supposed to emerge. She was going to be a tall, slender blonde, provocatively dressed. She would have the briefcase and possibly a second bag containing said laptop. She would most likely also have a purse.

Paco had already spent the past hour at various points along the street. He'd parked nearby two hours ago and examined the building from every possible angle. He'd even ventured inside the hotel and checked for anything that seemed out of place.

So far, nothing had triggered a warning.

Everyone was who they were supposed to be. He'd spent years conducting surveillance and was confident he hadn't missed anything.

Still, the money involved troubled him. It was the kind of cash that would allow him to pay off his medical bills and travel the world for six months, maybe more. Or he might even buy an old boat and just cruise around islands in the Caribbean and drink rum all day.

Paco chastised himself. He was spending money he hadn't even earned yet.

He brought his attention back to the task at hand.

A group of businessmen passed by the coffee shop. Paco imagined them eight hours from now, after the work was done, drunk and gambling. Perhaps taking part in some of the city's seedier offerings.

Paco himself looked like a businessman. He'd put on a tailored charcoal suit and sat with his cell phone in his hand, as if he were waiting for a colleague to join him. Although he was extremely muscular, the suit camouflaged his considerable physique. A custom-made shoulder holster was home to his gun, a Beretta 9mm.

A woman entered the coffee shop and glanced at him. He ignored her. The last thing he wanted was any kind of conversation. Paco heard her order some fancy drink with at least three names. Before him in his paper cup was simple black coffee.

So far it sat untouched.

Across the street, a uniformed doorman opened the hotel's front door and a blonde woman emerged. Paco narrowed his eyes and studied her. She had on a tiny black dress, wholly inappropriate for this time of day, high heels, and she carried three bags; a purse, a briefcase and a computer bag with a shoulder strap.

Paco couldn't see her eyes as she was wearing oversized sunglasses but he saw the angle of her face change and he knew she was looking across the street at him.

Not a good sign. That was an amateur move, through and through, Paco thought.

She walked away from the hotel and began to cross the street directly toward him.

Jesus, even worse, he thought. If someone was watching...

The luxury SUV, a black Cadillac Escalade came from Paco's right and was going at least twenty miles over the speed limit.

It slid into Paco's vision with astonishing speed.

The blonde had just enough time to look to her

left as the big vehicle slammed into her without slowing down.

Even through the glass windows of the coffee shop Paco could hear the sound of flesh and bone being obliterated by thousands of pounds of Detroit-made steel.

The blond woman's slender body went airborne and all three items in her possession flew in opposite directions.

Paco exploded from his chair and was out the door of the coffee shop in less than three seconds. The Beretta was in his hand.

The girl was already dead, he knew that. A human body can't withstand that kind of force and be bent in that many directions without the loss of life.

It simply wasn't possible.

But the briefcase and the laptop bag were still there on the street.

The Escalade skidded to a stop.

Paco hit the street at a dead run, the gun in both hands, held forward.

The first person to emerge from the SUV was the driver. He was a white guy with dark sunglasses and he wore a dark suit.

Paco shot him center mass, a double tap. The two rounds stopped him in his tracks and he sagged to the ground. The second man out of the Cadillac was a black guy, bald, with the same kind of black suit the driver had. Paco fired at him, but missed.

He got to the bags first and scooped them up.

The black man's first bullet hit him in the hip and spun him around. Paco landed on his side. However, he landed facing the shooter so he was able to bring the Beretta to bear. He fired and this time he didn't miss.

His bullet went high and sheered off the top of the black man's bald head. Blood sprouted like a lawn sprinkler coming to life.

Paco didn't wait to see what happened next.

He grabbed the briefcase, and with the laptop bag strapped across his shoulder he got to his feet and ran for his car, parked a block away. More shots rang out behind him and something punched him hard in the leg and in his abdomen. But by then, he made it to the corner and he ducked around it, unlocked his vehicle and dove inside.

He threw the bags in the passenger foot space, keyed the car's ignition and when the engine roared to life he pulled a U-turn and raced away.

Paco thought he heard more gunfire but couldn't be sure.

His hotel was on the other side of the city and he drove fast but efficiently, making sure no one was following him. He also didn't want to attract any cops with erratic driving.

He thought he could make it to the hotel.

Once there, he would make a call to a good friend of his. A legend within a group of freelance soldiers known by a nickname: the Department of Murder.

A guy named Michael Tallon.

CHAPTER 4

AS HE WOULD CONTEMPLATE it later, Tallon wasn't exactly sure why he went into town to have a beer.

Maybe he was lonely.

The love of his life, Lauren Pauling, was still back in New York tying up some loose ends with the business she had sold. Something about the firm's acquisition of a new client had piqued her interest. So she was staying in the Big Apple for a little longer than they had both planned.

Which left Tallon on his own.

After a lifetime of being alone, initially finding himself going solo felt very natural. Even, at times, downright good. He'd always enjoyed solitude and found peace in the mountains behind his little adobe ranch in his corner of the world – at the junction of

Nevada and California – a stone's throw from Death Valley.

So it was a bit of a surprise to him that after he'd worked out, answered a couple of emails regarding possible upcoming security opportunities and pulled out some chicken to grill later, he'd hopped into his SUV and driven into town.

Town was a little place called Independence Springs, Nevada, and it consisted of a main street, a quiet residential section, post office, city hall and a single combined school.

There wasn't much more other than a grocery store, drug store and a few mom-and-pop type businesses. None of the big chain stores like Walmart or Target had bothered with the small community, which made Tallon happy.

One of the few establishments was a little place in town called Rooster's. It was a classic western watering hole made of clapboard with a front porch and country music playing 24/7. There was sawdust on the wood floor and a few John Wayne movie posters.

An older couple sat in a booth along the far wall. They both looked up as Tallon entered.

He took a seat at the U-shaped bar and the bartender who Tallon thought was also the owner, emerged from the back of the room near the kitchen.

Tallon was fairly certain her name was Kate. She was probably in her late thirties or early forties. She was pretty, with a permanent expression of semi-skepticism laced with sardonic amusement. It was the kind of face that said, *I've seen it all and at this point, I'm able to see the humor in even the worst of situations.*

Tallon liked her, had even escorted a rude gentleman out of the bar many months back. He wondered if he liked her because he felt a kinship with her take on life. He too had seen it all. Maybe he didn't always see the humor in life like Kate appeared to, and maybe that's why he was here now, ordering a beer.

She set the frosted mug in front of him.

"Start a tab?" she asked.

"Nah," Tallon replied and slid a twenty across the bar to her. "Just here for a cold one."

Kate got his change. "Haven't seen you in here in awhile."

"Yeah."

She noted his short answer and turned.

"Work, you know," he said quickly, surprising himself with the desire to keep her in front of him, talking.

"Yeah, I sure do know." She smiled and he noticed her teeth, which were perfect, save for one incisor just a touch out of place. It was one of those cases where a slight imperfection made everything just right.

Behind her, Tallon noticed the older couple in the booth. The man was looking at him as he put down a cell phone. He'd either just ended a phone call or sent a text. Tallon wondered why he was looking at him and the old man looked away when their eyes met. The woman's face wore a look of concern and it looked like she was saying something under her breath to the old man. Maybe scolding him for something.

Tallon took a drink of his beer and relished how cold it was. His run this morning had been long and brutal. Nothing capped off a jog through Death Valley better than a frosted mug of draft beer.

"What's their story?" Tallon asked Kate, nodding his head toward the couple.

"Ben and Mary?" Kate asked without turning to look at the couple. "They've lived here forever. They come in at least three times a week, always sit in the same booth and order the same thing: one cheeseburger they split with a side of onion rings."

Tallon took another sip of his beer.

Kate must have noticed the tone of his question because she asked, "Why?"

He shrugged his shoulders. "Is Ben any relation to that wonderful guy I met the last time I was here?"

Tallon was referring to a big load of uselessness who'd slapped Kate on the ass and threatened more until Tallon taught him the importance of respecting women. A rather harsh lesson administered in the tavern's parking lot. If Tallon recalled correctly, he'd broken the thumb and index finger on each of the big man's hands.

"Not that I know of," Kate said. "But everyone knows everyone around here."

Tallon nodded. He had a bad feeling about it but he was enjoying his beer and even contemplating a second.

"You're kidding me," Kate said. Tallon smiled. He didn't even have to look. He glanced up at her and saw she was looking toward the bar's entrance.

She looked back at him.

"How did you know?"

Tallon smiled, set down his beer and looked over at the bar's newest customers. Two men. The first one, a giant of a man, was Tallon's former student from the session in the parking lot. The second man was about the same size but definitely younger. Probably a brother or a cousin.

"Doug, I don't want any trouble," Kate said.

Tallon was amused. Doug must have told his old

buddy Ben that if the guy who'd given him the beat down in the parking lot ever showed up again, to call him immediately.

Tallon looked back at Kate.

"When I'm done with them, I'll have another one of these," he said and slid off his barstool.

CHAPTER 5

ONE OF THE reasons for Lauren Pauling's success over the years, as both an FBI agent and the owner of a private investigative firm, was her ability to delegate.

She could be hands-off when she needed to be.

At the same time, when she was hands-on, she exerted a level of control that bordered on the extreme. No detail was too small and nothing was overlooked. She was all in.

When her firm had grown and was taking clients away from some of her much bigger rivals, the offers had started to come in. She'd resisted them until the granddaddy of them all had arrived and she simply could not say no.

The price tag made her an independently

wealthy woman who could choose to do whatever she wanted to with the rest of her life.

There had been some concern on her part that she would have trouble letting go once she sold her firm. She'd built it from scratch, after all. From the ground up it had all been her work, her strategies, and her instincts.

Surprisingly, she'd had no trouble moving on.

Until now.

The CEO of the firm that had purchased her company, a man named Karl Furlong, had invited her to an annual meeting. There, one of the emerging stars of the company had announced the acquisition of a huge client. But for Pauling, the news had been delivered with no shortage of red flags.

Information on the new client had been scant.

And the employee who'd landed the huge account, a man named Henry Torcher, had given off a vibe to Pauling that had only raised her concerns.

So now, she was on the elevator taking it to the top floor where Furlong's company, Global Strategic Services Inc., or GSS, was headquartered. Like her firm had been, it was headquartered in Manhattan. Unlike her company, which had only been a few blocks from her co-op on Barrow Street, the firm was in SoHo, so she'd taken a cab down.

Now, the elevator doors opened and she walked to the front desk where she introduced herself and said she had an appointment with Karl Furlong.

The woman spoke into her headset and smiled at Pauling. "You can go right on back," she said. "It's the corner office at the end of the hall."

Pauling already knew that but she smiled and walked down to the CEO's office. His private secretary nodded to her and she went into the big office. It was floor-to-ceiling windows with multimillion dollar views of the city. Furlong, a trim man with a Savile Row suit and Patek Philippe watch, stood as she entered. He hadn't been sitting at his desk, but instead, at a small conference table around which sat four chairs.

Pauling hesitated.

Because in one of the other chairs was Henry Torcher. His immense bulk was stuffed into a tailored suit and the smile on his face was not friendly in the least. It was predatory, Pauling realized. He had short, close-cropped blond hair, icy blue eyes and a fleshy face tinged with red.

"Hello," he said to her. "I understand you have some concerns."

She wasn't fazed by the intensity of his expression.

But underneath it was something else that Pauling could feel radiating out toward her.

It was rage.

CHAPTER 6

THE BEHEMOTH of a man now known to Tallon as "Doug" didn't approach him straightaway. Instead, he went over to the old couple and said something.

"You don't have to do this," Kate said to Tallon. He had stood and begun to walk toward the door. "I can call the cops."

"No need to," Tallon said over his shoulder as he walked toward the door.

The younger man glanced over at Doug to see if he should let Tallon pass.

The answer must have been in the affirmative because he stepped aside and gave Tallon a look that was probably supposed to be intimidating.

"Tell your buddy the bell is ringing for round two," Tallon said, and stepped out of the bar into the hot desert sunshine.

He stepped down into the parking lot and stood in the center of the space, facing back toward the bar. The door was flung open and Doug hurried out, convinced that his quarry was probably running away.

It seemed to Tallon that the first lesson hadn't sunk in. Doug should have known that Tallon had no intention of running.

"You," Doug said to him.

Tallon got a better look at him in the bright light and saw that his hands were still kind of mangled. The fingers hadn't grown back straight and he wondered if Doug could even make a fist.

He got his answer when the younger man stepped forward.

"Get him, Bradley," Doug said.

"Whoa, guys," Tallon said. He held up his hands. "Look – are you two related?"

The younger man looked back at his elder.

"What's it to you?" Doug asked.

"I'm just wondering if you've got a big family. Because when I do the same thing to him," he said, pointing at Bradley, "that I did to you," and he pointed at Doug, "will I have to keep doing it with a new family member every few months? Until I get to the end of the line?"

"Listen to this guy!" Bradley said. His ham-like

face bore an expression of disbelief. With a shake of his head he raised his fists and turned slightly to the side.

Tallon immediately knew his new adversary had done at least some boxing. He was on the balls of his feet. He'd turned no doubt so he'd be able to throw some jabs and save the giant right haymaker that would be intended to decapitate Tallon. It would be his favorite punch that he'd probably had great success with on drunks after closing time.

And then Tallon's cell phone rang.

It was in his front pocket and at that moment, Bradley forgot he was a boxer and instead, turned into a brawler. He charged forward with a pathetic jab and swung a huge right cross that took so long to arrive Tallon felt like he should have brought his beer with him so he'd have something to drink while he waited.

When the giant fist passed by Tallon's face like a freight train pulling into the station, Tallon stepped forward and threw a straight right that hit Bradley square in the mouth. Tallon felt the man's lips burst and the teeth cave in. Tallon could tell the younger man was surprised. His eyes widened and he stood straight up.

Everyone's got a plan until they get punched in the mouth, someone wise once said.

Tallon kicked straight out with his heavy, steel-toed boots and his heel landed on Bradley's knee cap. Tallon kicked straight through it and heard a sickening pop as the young man's knee ligaments snapped and tore.

The kid crumpled to the ground and from behind the younger man, Doug let out a painful bellow. Maybe he felt guilty for recruiting his younger family member into the same humiliating beat he'd received. Or maybe it was sympathy pain. Whatever the reason, Doug lowered his head. He charged Tallon who easily stepped aside, avoiding Doug's grasp, and clouted Doug on the back of the head as he went by.

Tallon figured the young man had a better chance of learning his lesson so he decided to leave him conscious. Instead, he turned his attention to his former pupil who was now whirling around in a cloud of dust.

Tallon faked the same kind of big right cross that Bradley had thrown but stopped it halfway and when Doug's hands went up, Tallon buried a wicked left uppercut into the bigger man's belly.

"Ooh," Doug said.

There clearly hadn't been any ab work done recently in Doug's workouts because Tallon's fist felt like it had connected all the way through the man's midsection and scraped his spinal cord.

Doug leaned forward and now Tallon brought his right fist back down and pivoted for a powerful uppercut that caught Doug under the chin and lifted him straight up. Tallon heard the man's teeth shatter and one of the fragments hit Tallon in the face.

He finally managed to hit me, Tallon thought with wry amusement.

Doug landed flat on his back.

"Good Lord," Kate said behind him.

Tallon turned and saw the bartender looking at the two big men on the ground. He pulled out his cell phone and frowned at the caller ID.

Paco? he thought.

"I'll take a rain check on that second beer," Tallon told Kate. "Tell Ben he shouldn't have called them."

She smiled at him, the tired humor still on display in her eyes.

"Will do," she said.

CHAPTER 7

"NOW, I understand you have some questions about our new client, Zeta Corporation," Furlong said.

They had already dispensed with small talk and when it was clear there was a certain amount of unease at the table, the CEO had decided to get to the heart of the matter.

"Not exactly concern," Pauling said. Inwardly, she was displeased Furlong had chosen to invite Torcher for the meeting. She had really meant it to be a very unofficial chat during which she had been planning to simply mention, as an aside, her questions regarding the news of the new account.

"Then what?" Torcher asked. He leaned forward in his chair, his massive shoulders straining against the custom-made shirt – probably designed to show off his bodybuilder's physique. His face had taken on an even dark tint of red. Anger? Steroids? Testosterone injections? Pauling wondered.

"Well, as I mentioned at the annual meeting it seemed that background information on Zeta was scant," she said. "You, I believe, had said you would follow up with more details."

Pauling let the sentence end with the implication hanging in the air. Torcher certainly hadn't followed up with any more information.

"Yes, I apologize for that," he said. "I've got a new team working on this account and although I had directed them to get you that information, clearly, they hadn't followed through. I will remedy that immediately."

"Thank you," Pauling said.

Karl Furlong cocked his head and raised an eyebrow at Pauling. "Is that the only reason you contacted me? A lack of background information?"

This was getting to the heart of the matter and Pauling would certainly have to tread lightly. If it was her company, she wouldn't have had to bother with such niceties.

"Now that you mention it, the numbers presented were quite large. Almost staggeringly so," she said.

Torcher beamed a megawatt smile at Furlong. "Indeed," he said.

"Having worked in the private security sector for so long, it surprised me that a company with that kind of budget was one I had never heard of," Pauling said. "As you know, when I was at the helm of my company new account acquisitions were something I focused on. So, at one point or another, I had at least initial contact with virtually every large company with a significant need for security in the world. Yet, somehow, I had never heard of Zeta Corporation."

Pauling omitted the fact that she had done some initial online research, admittedly superficial, and found virtually nothing save for a minimalist website and a few listings on various business association databases.

Torcher's big head swiveled directly at Pauling.

"First off, I don't know if I mentioned this already, but I wanted to thank you for bringing your concerns to Karl," Torcher said. "Your dedication is a big reason we're all sitting here today and the fact that you continue to remain invested in the firm's success is admirable."

Pauling's bullshit meter was in full red alarm but her face remained impassive.

"Thank you," she said.

"Now, let me tell you about Zeta Corporation. There is a very good reason for the limited information available to the public. They are, in fact, also in the security sector. However, unlike our services, which tend to be investigation, surveillance, personal protection and so on, they are purely digital security."

"So, software?" Pauling asked.

"More than that, although software is certainly a key component of their portfolio. They have expanded into all things related to our electronic lives, in every sense of the term. Software, hardware, mobile, social and now the very exciting field of artificial intelligence. So much of what they do is classified, you can certainly understand their need for privacy."

"When you say classified I assume you mean they are also working with various governments?"

Torcher nodded his oversized cranium. "They are."

"Where are they headquartered?" Pauling asked.

"Munich."

Furlong smiled. "The Germans are second only to the Swiss for their love of privacy."

Pauling wasn't so sure that was a good thing.

"Do they have a CEO?"

"Yes," Torcher said. "Her name is Becher. Goda Becher."

For the first time, Pauling second-guessed her instincts on Zeta. Now she had a name and a location.

"Also, Zeta is part of a fairly significant meeting among a large group of vendors, employees and other important industry leaders next week in Los Angeles," Torcher said. "We would be delighted if you would attend. Then you would probably learn more about Zeta than you ever wanted to."

Even better, Pauling thought. There was no way they would invite her if Torcher and Zeta had something to hide.

Furlong must have sensed her change in attitude.

"Now, do you have any more questions for Henry? He's got a lot on his plate right now, as you can imagine."

"No, I don't want to keep you from your work."

She smiled at Torcher and they all stood. He held out his hand and she shook it. His grip was ferociously strong and he gave it an extra squeeze.

Pauling felt a twinge of pain and just as suddenly, he let go.

"I will have all of Zeta's paperwork immediately couriered to your home," Torcher said. There was a curious light in his eyes and Pauling disliked the idea he knew where she lived.

"Perfect," Pauling said.

Even to her own ears, she didn't sound very convincing.

CHAPTER 8

TWO FOR TWO.

Two times he'd gone to Rooster's for a beer and twice he'd wound up in the parking lot providing locals lessons on etiquette.

Well, there wouldn't be a third time, Tallon thought. As much as he occasionally enjoyed slipping into town for a beer, it just wasn't worth it. Because he liked Kate, the owner. She seemed like a straight shooter.

He was on his way back home, pleased there wasn't a cop in pursuit. He knew Kate wouldn't call the police on him and the two thugs he'd knocked around probably wouldn't either.

That was good. He didn't have anything against cops, heck, often times his jobs in various parts of the world could almost be deemed law enforcement. No, he just simply wished to lead a quiet life, which is why he'd chosen Independence Springs in the first place. He had enough action and violence in his day job, he didn't need that at home, too.

Now, he pressed his cell phone to his ear and played back Paco's voicemail message.

Except, it really wasn't much of a message.

Tallon heard the sound of breathing. Paco coughed a couple of times. Maybe there was a whisper and then that was it.

Tallon frowned.

That was very unlike Paco. The Paco he knew was sharp, direct and no-nonsense. He was also one of the best operatives he'd ever worked with.

The hell with this, Tallon thought. He tapped the callback button and put the phone back to his ear.

His call went straight to Paco's voicemail.

"Hey, it's me. Call me back."

Tallon disconnected from the call and turned the volume on his phone all the way up.

He played back the voicemail message.

And then he played it again.

The last time, he heard a little bit differently. Tallon pressed the SUV's accelerator to the floor and raced back to his casita. He drove into the garage, parked, and went inside. He shut the door to his office and hooked his phone to his office's sound system and then put it full volume. There were six high-definition speakers placed strategically around the room as well as a powerful subwoofer.

He listened again.

This time, the sound quality was much better and the detail was much clearer.

"Shit."

Just like that, Tallon knew Paco was dead.

Because those two coughs hadn't come from his friend.

They'd come from a handgun fitted with a silencer.

They no doubt were the shots that killed Paco.

Held by the killer who was the reason Paco had called.

Tallon unplugged his phone and scrolled through his contacts until he found a friend who could trace a cell phone call.

Tallon was going to find out where Paco was when he made that call.

And then he was going to go there.

And if Paco was dead, Tallon was going to find out who killed him.

And return the favor.

CHAPTER 9

PAULING CHECKED HER WATCH.

Tallon was three hours behind her, so she decided to wait and call him closer to his dinner time.

After her meeting with Furlong and Torcher, Pauling had gone to her gym and worked out. Even though she wasn't operating in the field anymore, that didn't necessarily mean she never would again. Staying in good physical condition was essential. Especially at her age. She was older than most of the women at the gym, but she prided herself on being among the best in terms of fitness.

She'd made it in time to do her forty-five minute cycling class and then after that she'd done a circuit on the weight machines. Free weights were better for her, but sometimes she liked the prearranged structure of the machines. The cycling session had kicked her ass anyway, so a hardcore strength session wasn't the goal.

With her workout complete, she left the gym and picked up where her thoughts had left off. Namely, what exactly was the next chapter in her life going to be?

Since she'd sold her company, more and more she'd been thinking about exactly what she wanted in her life and perhaps just as importantly, what she didn't.

Not long after the sale went through, her sister had been abducted. Luckily, she and Tallon, along with the help of a private investigator in Florida, had been able to find her and return her to her family.

Now that she thought about it, Pauling contemplated if she went to Los Angeles, maybe she would catch a flight up to Portland afterward and check on her sister. Readjusting to something like what her sister had been put through could take time and be extremely difficult. Pauling wanted to be there for her sister to help with the transition back to a normal life. Well, as normal as it could be. Her sister, her family, would probably never be the same.

Now, Pauling returned to her co-op on Barrow Street, keyed in the code to her loft and stepped inside. Not long ago she'd had a state-of-the-art security system installed after someone had broken in and planted listening devices in her home.

That wouldn't happen again.

Pauling set her purse on the kitchen table, opened the fridge and dug out a bottle of white wine. She poured herself a glass and browsed through the mail.

Nothing of importance. Everything was set up on AutoPay and her bills were handled electronically. She'd been spending so much time with Tallon out west that her life here had slowed dramatically.

She'd noticed there was virtually no food in the refrigerator, not even leftovers. Pauling weighed her options – go out to a restaurant? Or get creative?

She took her glass of wine into the living room and settled into the couch. Her home was a good reflection of her personality; stylish, comfortable and modern. Her furnishings were simple but high-quality and everything was in its place.

The intercom came to life with news she had a delivery. Pauling set down her wine and retrieved the package. She noted the return label showed it had originated from Global Strategic Services. It must be the paperwork on Zeta Corporation Torcher had promised her.

She tore open the envelope and was surprised to see there was only a slim folder.

She opened the folio and saw it was a travel itinerary. A first-class ticket to Los Angeles and three nights at a swanky hotel in Beverly Hills.

Pauling checked the rest of the envelope.

No information included on Zeta.

Hadn't Torcher said he was going to send it along with information regarding the conference in LA? Had he forgotten? Or had he once again refused to provide what she had asked for?

Pauling sighed.

Corporate America could be like this, she knew firsthand. Say one thing in a meeting and then afterward, do something completely different. Office politics never died.

Still, it was a trip to LA. From there she could either go to Portland and see her sister or it was close enough that she could just drive to Independence Springs and rejoin Tallon.

Pauling sat down again and sipped her wine.

There was no way Torcher had simply forgotten to provide the information she'd requested. It was an obvious oversight. Done purposely.

The only thing Pauling didn't know, was why?

CHAPTER 10

NOT MUCH CAN MAKE a man feel old than when his friends start dying. For Tallon, he'd seen many of his buddies die violent deaths and now he feared Paco was a new addition to that macabre list.

Still, he didn't know for certain Paco was dead. Maybe those silenced gunshots were fired *by* Paco, not *at* him. Maybe his old buddy had his hands full with something and would call Tallon later.

It didn't seem that way, though. His guess was that Paco had been wounded, called Tallon for help and then whoever was pursuing him finally fired two rounds to end the story.

Tallon paced inside his home office. He had several computers as well as his home security system set up inside the space. Mostly, he needed to find out where Paco was when he'd called. He needed a starting point.

No message had arrived yet from his friend who had the ability to trace cell phone calls, so Tallon went out to the kitchen, pulled a beer from the fridge and stepped out onto the back patio.

In the distance, the last glimmer of sunlight was fading behind the mountains and the shadows were slowly walking their way toward him. He sat in one of the chairs that faced the fire pit and contemplated throwing some logs together and lighting them up, but chose not to.

He wasn't in the mood.

A dark night without warmth and an encroaching chill seemed more appropriate.

Tallon thought about texting Pauling but also decided not to. Deep down, he knew what was bothering him. He was feeling old and wondered if Paco's possible death had been caused in part because his friend was getting old, too. Maybe Paco had been slowing down. He'd lost a step or two, as they liked to say.

It happened to the best of soldiers. Oftentimes, it took one bad mission, a failure to perform at the level to which they'd grown accustomed, to convince once elite warriors to admit it was time to call it quits.

Tallon wasn't there yet.

But maybe he would be. Sooner than later.

His phone buzzed in his front pocket and he pulled it out.

On the screen was a simple message:

Vegas. Best guess: the Landmark Hotel or very close by.

So Paco had been in Vegas. The fact caused mixed emotions. He was glad it was close by, but also felt guilt that his former comrade-in-arms had been so close and clearly in need of help.

He'd never heard of the Landmark Hotel but he wasn't surprised. Hotels were going out of business and then reopening under a new name all the time in Las Vegas.

Tallon also knew that tracing a cell phone call wasn't a totally exact science. But his friend was good with triangulating and if he suggested the hotel, it was probably the right place.

He drank his beer and thought about his schedule. He wasn't sure what Pauling was doing. Tallon hoped she would be coming back soon.

His next job was two months away and would be in Africa. At least a two-month stint providing security for an American geologic company and their personnel.

Which meant he had plenty of time for a trip to Vegas to see what the hell was going on with Paco.

Tallon would just have to close up the little ranch, set the security system and pack up his gear. He went back into the house through the kitchen and into a highly secure room that served as his armory.

If, in fact, the gunshots had been silenced that meant Paco was dealing with someone who was a professional. And if this person had managed to take down a man Tallon knew to be one of the best, then the danger he might face in Sin City was very real.

He looked at the guns in the cabinets and on the wall and chose two handguns, each fitted with sound suppressors, plenty of ammunition for them, as well as an MP5 submachine gun. Tallon considered bringing one of his sniper rifles but ultimately decided against it. This felt like something that would require close-quarters work.

Satisfied with his choices he went into his bedroom and began to pack.

He was glad that it was a relatively short drive and wouldn't require a flight, which would complicate the transportation of weapons.

As he packed, he felt conflicted by another emotion.

Guilt.

Paco was probably dead and *now* he was going to show up.

The damage had been done, most likely.

Well, it wasn't totally done, at least not the damage he intended to inflict.

CHAPTER 11

PAULING HAD NEVER BEEN a fantastic sleeper.

In fact, she was a bit of a legend at the Bureau for her ability to function at a high level despite having only a couple hours of sleep at night. Since she'd gone into the private sector, she'd definitely changed her habit of going on limited sleep. It just hadn't been necessary.

Perhaps it was due to the envelope and Torcher's obvious reluctance to divulge any more information on Zeta Corporation that had caused Pauling to stare at her bedroom ceiling well into the night.

Now, bright and early, she rose, poured herself a cup of coffee (the machine was set on a timer) and thought about her day ahead. The flight to Los Angeles left in the early evening, so she had plenty of time to pack and get to the airport.

Pauling thought about texting her sister but since she and her family lived in Portland, they were a full three hours behind. Instead, Pauling busied herself with packing as well as clearing her email and other minor tasks.

Later, when it was a more reasonable hour, she sent her sister a message.

She offered to pop up to Portland after the conference in Los Angeles. Pauling hoped her sister said yes. Sometimes after a traumatic ordeal like her sister endured, victims felt insecure and indecisive.

When her phone vibrated, Pauling had to smile.

Actually, we're going to be away. How about closer to the holidays?

Her sister had always been direct and clearly she remained as decisive as she'd always been, which made Pauling feel relieved.

She tapped out a response saying that sounded great, and then called Tallon.

"Hey," she said when he answered.

"Hey right back."

"What are you up to?"

"I'm actually on my way to Vegas."

"The airport?" She knew Tallon usually flew out of the Vegas airport when he needed to travel for work. "Or a casino?"

"Ha," he said. "Um, neither. A buddy called and might need my help."

She caught the change in tone and knew it might not be something he wanted to talk about over the phone.

"Okay."

"How 'bout you?" he asked.

"On my way to Los Angeles for a meeting regarding my old firm's newest client."

"The mysterious one?"

"Yes, indeed. That's the one. Apparently, I'm going to learn all I ever wanted to know about Zeta Corporation. I figured after that, I could swing by your place."

She had almost called it "home" but neither one of them was at that point just yet.

"Do you think you'll be back by then?" she asked.

"Probably. But I'll keep you posted."

They talked for a few more minutes, ended the call with matching "love yous" and then Pauling disconnected.

She hoped he would be back by then. Otherwise, she'd have to decide between going to his place when he wasn't here or coming back to New York.

Well, it was something she could put off until then.

For now, she had a plane to catch.

CHAPTER 12

DISPOSING of dead bodies was never his thing.

Turning living human beings into dead bodies, however, was.

It was something he was very, very good at.

It's why he'd earned the nickname "Sino" which was an abbreviation of the Spanish word for assassin: Asesino.

Now, Sino was disgusted. He'd watched as the lower-level team, whose job it had been to grab the blonde hooker along with the briefcase and laptop bag, had totally botched it. He'd almost enjoyed watching them get gunned down by the operative known as Paco. It didn't matter that they had technically been a part of his team. Sino hated sloppy work and it was better they die now than later.

Oh, Sino had done his homework. He'd been semi-impressed with Paco's shooting.

It had almost been a shame to slip into his adversary's hotel room and put two bullets in the man's head. The man had already been wounded, so in some ways Sino considered it a bit of a coup de grace. Not much of a challenge. At this point in his career, Sino liked the occasional challenge. He liked money most of all but sometimes he got bored.

Understandably, he'd been a bit pissed off when word had come down that since the rest of the team had been killed in the shootout outside the hotel, it was now up to Sino to get rid of the body and retrieve the evidence.

He'd reached a certain level in his profession where "getting one's hands dirty" was over.

Sino had not forgotten how to do it, though.

He simply went down to the hotel's laundry room, snagged a cart, brought it back up to the hotel room and dumped the body inside. He covered it in towels to stop any blood seepage that might attract attention.

He'd brought his own Cadillac Escalade around to the back of the hotel where the little loading area was for linens and kitchen supplies. It was empty and the heavy door was unlocked.

He brought the cart back down, rolled it right off the ramp and into the back of the SUV.

From there he drove out into the desert.

So many places to dump a body out here, Sino thought. Plus, he had all-wheel drive with the big SUV even though no one on God's green earth would consider the Cadillac an off-road vehicle.

Sino was tired and thirsty. He'd forgotten to bring some water which was just plain stupid. You always have water when you go into the desert. The hell with water, Sino thought.

What he really wanted was tequila.

Killing a man always initiated a desire for booze and sex. He would have to pick up a bottle of the good stuff and then find a prostitute back in Vegas as soon as he was done.

And he intended to waste no time in doing so.

He turned off the main road via a dim trail that might have belonged to some kind of park service and as soon as he was hidden from view he parked, opened the back of the SUV and rolled the cart out of the vehicle. It crashed into the dirt and the body partially spilled out.

Sino grabbed the dead man by the ankles and dragged him off the trail to the edge of the ditch and then pushed it with his foot until it rolled down into the gulley.

Sino wished he'd brought something to cover the body but all that was left was the cart and a bunch of blood-stained towels.

Ah, what the hell, he thought. He tossed the towels down on top of the dead man and rolled the cart off to the other side of the trail. Sino closed up the vehicle and drove back to the highway.

His plan was to go back to a bar in town and order the most expensive tequila they had. But his thirst had grown immensely. Just down the road was a shabby little liquor store.

It would have to do until he made it back into Sin City.

CHAPTER 13

TALLON SMILED as the call with Pauling ended.

He never tired of hearing her voice; that wonderful raspiness that sounded like whiskey and cigarettes in a jazz bar.

Tallon wished he'd been able to tell her how long he'd be in Vegas. Unfortunately, he didn't know how long he'd be there. It all depended upon what he would find.

For now, it felt good to be back on the road. He wished it were under better circumstances.

As he drove, Tallon thought about Paco. One of the toughest guys he'd ever known. Physically, Paco was ridiculously strong. Few guys could compete with him when it came to deadlifting serious weight.

Fearless under fire, too. Tallon recalled a firefight in Afghanistan when he and Paco were working as private security. This was between the two wars. They'd run into a pocket of foreign fighters and had to shoot their way out. Paco had not only kept his cool, but seemed to enjoy the precariousness of their situation. Tallon had been severely impressed with the man. In an intense firefight there was no man Tallon would rather have next to him than Paco Williams.

So what had happened to him in Vegas?

Tallon subconsciously drove faster and soon the freeway crested a small rise and there before him lay the city of Las Vegas.

From the highway, it didn't look much like the famous images paraded around the Internet. Tallon was certainly used to a desert climate, but the combination of traffic and brown landscape left him less than enthused. He was nonplussed by it, though. For one thing, it was his main hub for air travel. He probably came into town once a month.

It was also like any other city – nothing looked all that great from a freeway. You had to get into the heart of things to find out what a town was really like.

With that in mind, Tallon tapped his navigation system into which he'd already entered the Landmark Hotel as its destination.

He followed its directions and within ten

minutes he was driving past the hotel. He hit the "end" button on the nav system and drove on past. It was a fairly elegant hotel by Vegas standards. Probably what they called a "boutique" hotel these days. It was a contemporary white tower with mirrored windows and a coral-colored Art Deco-inspired façade. It gave off a vibe of being retro but not in a hackneyed way, which is how things were usually done in Vegas.

There was no casino attached. Tallon was glad for that. A casino meant tons of foot traffic and innocent civilians wandering around.

Tallon drove around the block and cruised past the hotel again. He studied it looking for any watchers. People who didn't belong. The area looked clean and he wondered if Paco had thought the same thing. It was easy to get lulled into being relaxed.

Tallon had no intention of making that mistake.

Finally satisfied with his initial assessment, he parked two blocks down and walked back.

He entered the hotel and was hit by the fresh scent of lemons. There was a huge water pitcher filled with them on a long, rectangular table made of black lacquered wood. The Art Deco motif continued inside with framed travel posters from the twenties. A light fixture made of recycled martini glasses added a touch of whimsy to the entrance. The tile floor was black-and-white checked and finely polished. The lobby was cavernous, surprisingly so, considering its exterior which communicated a boutique aesthetic.

A sweeping western mural occupied one wall and on the other, a wall of glass.

Ahead, a front desk was partially obscured by a fountain shooting plumes of water in unison.

Tallon had come prepared with a photo of Paco. He stepped up to the front desk and explained that his friend, Paco Williams had invited him for a drink. Could the front desk ring his room and let him know he was here?

The front desk employee was a young woman with dark black hair, caramel-colored skin and she wore a white suit with a black vest.

"Of course," she said.

She tapped the keys of a computer and frowned. "We don't have a guest here by that name."

"Really? This is the Landmark Hotel, right?"

"Yes it is. Did he possibly register under a different name?"

"No, Paco Williams. P-A-C-O. Williams as it's always spelled."

She tried again but to no avail.

Tallon pulled out the photograph and showed it to her.

"Hmm. He does look familiar," she said. "But we have a lot of guests in and out of here every day. Would you like me to get my manager? Although, honestly, I don't think there's anything we can do."

Tallon shook his head.

"No, but I would like to check in, if you have a room available."

"We do," she said and smiled, happy she could at least accommodate something he wished for.

Tallon retrieved his bags and went to his room. It was on the sixth floor. Very chic with a steel-and-black leather desk chair, a purple lounge chair and a king bed featuring an ultra-modern headboard.

Tallon set his bags on the bed, used the restroom and then stood and looked out the window. Beyond, he could see the famous Vegas strip.

He'd checked in for one reason only.

This was where Paco had made the call. He knew that because of the woman at the front desk. She had, in fact, recognized Paco. Her look gave it away and when she tried to recover from her mistake, she'd only made it worse.

It was all the confirmation Tallon had needed.

Now, he had one goal in mind.

Figure out which room he'd stayed in.

CHAPTER 14

THOUSANDS OF MILES away a man sat and watched his computer.

He'd just watched in real-time as the front desk terminal at the Landmark Hotel in Las Vegas had processed a search for a guest named Paco Williams.

The man sitting in front of the computer knew that Paco Williams had, in fact, been a guest at the hotel.

He also knew that any record of the man's stay had thoroughly and systematically been erased from the hotel's records. He himself had not been the one who had performed the operation, he'd simply watched as it happened before his very eyes.

The man crossed his arms and a tattoo flashed under the blue light of the computer monitor. It was an image of a snake's head with oversized hinged fangs.

When colleagues had dubbed the man "Viper" for the speed and aggressiveness of his intellect, he'd followed up one drunken night by impetuously getting the tattoo. He'd regretted it ever since but hadn't taken the steps to get the damn thing removed. For now, he was just living with it.

Despite his legendary reputation for computer virtuosity, he was doing nothing at the moment other than simply staring at his screen.

And thinking.

Mainly, he was thinking about how he may have been responsible for several murders. Everything had suddenly become terrifyingly real. These weren't computer simulations; artificial entities dying in pretend cyberspace. This was real human blood being shed.

And his hands were covered with it.

He couldn't think about that now.

The man known as Viper had to do something and do it fast.

Or more people were going to die.

Many, many more.

CHAPTER 15

PAULING SAT in the first class section of the direct flight from New York to LA. They'd already lifted off and she had a glass of chardonnay on the foldout desktop. Next to her was a cosmetic dentist who was going to LA. for a conference on new and innovative uses of dental veneers. It sounded dreadfully boring to Pauling, but *each to his own*, she thought.

Having already exhausted as much dentistry conversation as she wished, Pauling opened her laptop and connected to the airplane's Wi-Fi. She'd long ago purchased the access for herself and found it to be extremely useful.

Today was no exception.

She was a big believer in research and there was no way she was going to walk into a conference ostensibly to learn more about the Zeta Corporation without doing her due diligence. Pauling had thoroughly depleted the first line of research which had consisted of basic Internet searches as well as premium business-related websites which contained private information for investors.

The results had been disappointing to say the least.

It had occurred to her that perhaps she ought to make a foray into the next level of scrutiny; namely, professional researchers with special abilities to navigate security measures designed to keep them out.

Her go-to researcher was a Canadian who had originally emigrated from somewhere in Europe. He was expensive, but worth every penny.

Pauling fired up her private email account and sent him a message with a simple request for everything he could find on Zeta Corporation whose headquarters were possibly in Munich, Germany, which is what Henry Torcher had told her in the meeting at Global Security Solutions.

Pauling also sent her researcher the name of Goda Becher, the woman Torcher had told her was the CEO of Zeta.

This was particularly intriguing because Pauling's own research had failed to bring up any mention anywhere of a woman named Goda Becher.

How had she managed to become head of a

company whose budget was as enormous as Torcher claimed, yet leave no trace anywhere of her existence?

As an afterthought, she also asked her researcher to find out what she could about Henry Torcher. The man had piqued her interest as well. Pauling realized she didn't know how long he'd been with Karl Furlong and GSS and, for that matter, where he'd come from.

With that complete, Pauling closed her email.

She launched her web browser to the most neutral website she could find and read the headlines. The economy was still going strong. A European soccer player was being accused of sexual assault. And a Silicon Valley executive had been murdered in Las Vegas. A man named Mikael Gladhus.

Pauling read the story intensely even though the name was not familiar to her.

Las Vegas.

Where Tallon was headed.

To help a friend, he'd said.

She made a mental note to text him when they landed. The two things – the man's murder and Tallon's trip to Las Vegas – certainly weren't related.

One never knew, she thought.

Stranger things had happened.

murdered nearby, around the same time that Paco had been in enough trouble to call Tallon? And leave a strange voicemail that sounded suspiciously like someone firing a pistol with a sound suppressor attached?

And now, Paco was nowhere to be found? And if he was dead, why had no one found his body?

Tallon didn't have any answers. He finished his beer and ordered another one.

He wasn't a big believer in coincidences. He knew Paco worked a lot of high-profile security jobs. Maybe he'd been brought in to work for this Gladhus guy? Maybe the same person responsible for Gladhus' murder had taken out Paco at the same time?

He grabbed his phone and scrolled to the mobile browser. Tallon again read the story of Gladhus' murder and saw that it had taken place in front of a place called Empire. It occurred to him that if Paco had come into town to work security for Gladhus, taking a room at the Landmark would have been convenient and close.

Tallon left his second beer half-finished, paid the tab and walked out of the hotel. He strolled down toward the location of Empire, which he guessed was another luxury hotel.

The night was hot and dry. Ahead, he could see the lights of Vegas proper. He could practically smell the tourists eager to make the most of the time in the city. No doubt working hard to do things that would make for great stories when they returned home to suburbia U.S.A.

Who could blame them? Life was short. Tallon knew that more than anyone.

Now, he got to Empire's entrance and saw that it was indeed another hotel. Like the Landmark, it didn't seem like a casino was attached.

Tallon walked past the entrance to Empire and kept walking. He went to the end of the block, crossed the street and stopped at the coffee shop directly across from Empire. If he were a betting man, this would have been where Paco had stationed himself. Easy to blend in. A safe distance. Depending, of course, on what his mission had been.

Tallon left the coffee shop and crossed the street. He entered Empire's lobby and went to the front desk. This hotel made no pretense at historical references. It was uber contemporary and ultra chic. Tallon guessed the rooms were significantly more expensive than the Landmark.

The front desk was manned by a powerfully built blond man with a gap in his front tooth. Tallon repeated the question about Paco and showed the photograph.

The man shook his head.

"I don't believe I've ever seen him here," he said.

Tallon thanked him, left Empire and walked back outside.

So far, he hadn't learned much.

Except for one thing.

Someone else was interested in Paco.

Because Tallon had picked up a follower. He was being watched, and from the looks of it, by more than one person.

CHAPTER 17

THE PLANE ARRIVED in Los Angeles on time. The flight from New York had been uneventful.

The dentist seated next to Pauling allowed her to exit the plane first. He followed her down to baggage claim but did not stand next to her. Instead, once she'd retrieved her bag, he followed her out to the area designated Ground Transportation. A car was there waiting for her.

Once she took a seat and the car drove off, he took out his phone.

"It's me," he said. "She sent an email to someone. I couldn't read the whole message but I saw the names Zeta, Becher and maybe Henry."

He paused and listened.

"No, I couldn't make out the email address."

With the phone pressed to his ear he walked

down to where the taxicabs were waiting. He got in line.

"Yes, I understand," he said.

When his cab arrived he climbed in and told the driver the name of the hotel.

It would be good to watch this Lauren Pauling again, he thought to himself.

If the need arose, he hoped he would be chosen to eliminate her. She was good-looking and he loved her voice. Sort of like Kathleen Turner but even better looking. A sexy older woman he could really sink his teeth into.

He smiled at the joke.

Dentist, indeed.

CHAPTER 18

UNLIKE NINETY PERCENT of the folks who visit Las Vegas every year, they were the exception. Maybe because they were older. Or because they had raised a family and were now proud grandparents.

Or, more accurately, it was probably because they were both professors. In particular, the woman was a geology professor who loved nothing more than to venture north of Las Vegas and spend time in the legendary landscape. Oh sure, they didn't mind the occasional show, but they had little time for the casinos, gamblers and overpriced unhealthy buffet dinners.

No, they actually enjoyed the land itself the most. In particular, the woman was quite fond of north-south faults and the large amount of alluvial deposits.

Today, though, they were mostly walking for pleasure. They each had a pair of hiking sticks and plenty of water. At their age, staying hydrated was essential, much more important than the typical hikers who were at least two or three decades younger.

One other thing separated them from the hikers in their twenties and thirties. Namely, they tended to stray from the trail.

The woman in particular was more interested in the rocks and sediments that were off trail, perhaps washed there by rains over the years. So she tended to hike some twenty to thirty yards on either side of the trail, terrain permitting.

In this stretch of this particular canyon that was possible. Although there was a steep drop-off, there was no vegetation or formidable rock structure to impede her path.

No, the only thing she saw ahead was some trash someone had clearly dumped. It was stark white in contrast to the land and she approached it with a vague sense of anger. She hated it when people polluted the natural landscape. And clearly, they'd dumped a lot of garbage because as they came closer she could see a group of vultures were feasting on what was inside.

She rejoined her husband on the main trail, and as they walked past the birds they averted their eyes.

But not before the husband spotted an item in one of the vulture's claws.

It was a human hand.

CHAPTER 19

TALLON WAS NOT BEING PARANOID. He'd never been one to exaggerate or diminish threats. His life had been one long training program designed to teach him how to recognize danger and neutralize it.

So the man at the other end of the street, waiting at the bus stop for a supposed ride, was not really a bus rider. Tallon knew that.

For one, he'd seen the man before. When Tallon had been in the coffee shop, he'd walked past, a cell phone to his ear. Tallon had noted the man's casual wardrobe; jeans, a black sweatshirt and black boots. Nothing special.

Now, the same man was waiting for a bus. Which begged the question why had he been walking in the other direction less than ten minutes ago? The obvious answer: he'd simply walked around the block.

The other watcher was a woman. She had on a cream-colored pantsuit and carried a large purse. She wore aviator sunglasses and her hair was swept back into a tight bun.

She was drinking coffee from a Styrofoam cup and waiting outside an office building three doors down from the hotel. To the casual observer, it would appear she possibly had a meeting with a company inside the building and was perhaps waiting for a coworker to appear or maybe killing time before her meeting.

Nothing about her was a dead giveaway to Tallon.

No, nothing obvious. But the reason Tallon had pegged her as a watcher was the same reason he'd decided the guy waiting for the bus had him under surveillance.

They were both carrying guns.

No matter how slim-fitting a holster was, or how small a handgun could be, the human body adjusted to its presence. Tallon knew the man with the black sweatshirt had a fairly high-caliber pistol on his right side. It was simply by the way the man carried himself.

The woman was different. She had a weapon in

her purse. Tallon knew right away by the way she positioned it against her body.

He sighed and crossed the street. No sense in hurrying back to his hotel. Besides, now he knew with absolute certainty he was in the right place.

Tallon went into the coffee shop and approached the barista; a willowy man with a scraggly goatee and sleepy eyes. His name tag read "Dale."

"What can I get you?" he asked, with as much enthusiasm as he could muster which turned out to be virtually none.

"A small black coffee and an answer."

"An answer? To what?"

Tallon pulled out the photograph of Paco. "If you saw this man recently."

Dale had placed a paper cup under a giant cylinder and steaming hot coffee poured into it. Now, he leaned back toward Tallon and glanced at the photograph.

"Yeah he was here," Dale said. "Until that weird prank went down."

Tallon raised an eyebrow. "Prank?"

Dale placed the coffee on the counter and took Tallon's five-dollar bill. Tallon waved his hand to say, keep the change.

"Thanks," Dale said. "Yeah. Yesterday there was some kind of loud commotion. Sounded like gunshots. I was working and could see someone fall down and then everyone got into these black SUVs and sped off. I figured it was a prank or maybe a movie. They shoot movies around here all the time. You never know what's real or not, but that's Vegas, right?"

"Did you see any cameras?"

"No."

"Did the cops show up?"

"Yep. They even asked me what happened and I told them. One of them said there was some blood on the sidewalk but that was it. I told them to see if there were any security cameras around. Maybe some footage."

"Good idea," Tallon said. There was more to Dale than met the eye. He was probably a fan of true crime shows. There were a lot of them on Netflix nowadays.

"Then what happened?"

"Nothing. No one came back to talk to me. I didn't see anything on the news – except that some guy was killed in that same hotel but in his room. Which is a weird coincidence. But again this is Vegas, man. Anything can happen, and usually does."

Tallon picked up his coffee.

He held up the picture of Paco.

"What else can you tell me about him?"

"Not much. He had a small black coffee just like you. He left just before all that commotion happened and then I thought I saw him go that way."

Dale pointed in the general direction of the Landmark Hotel.

Tallon took a sip of his coffee.

"Good stuff," he said.

"Organic. From Nigeria. Best coffee in the world, in my opinion."

"Thanks for the coffee and the info." Tallon handed him a business card. "Call me if you think of anything else. I'm staying just up the street at the Landmark."

"Yeah, no problem," Dale said. "I hope you find your friend."

Me too, Tallon thought.

He walked out of the coffee shop and wondered if the blood on the sidewalk had been Paco's or someone else's.

Tallon started back toward his hotel.

His watchers followed.

CHAPTER 20

PAULING HAD SPENT enough time in Los Angeles to know the character of its different regions. For instance, she'd worked, shopped and dined along the ocean in Santa Monica where the promenade was a beehive of tourists and occasional locals. Lots of buskers and beggars as well.

Out in Malibu Pauling had spent a weekend surfing with a fellow FBI agent. He was a California native and he and Pauling had been an item for a few brief months way back when she first joined the Bureau. It had been a memorable weekend and he'd taken her to a lot of his favorite Malibu haunts.

Much later she'd returned and worked a case in Beverly Hills. It had been a drug smuggling operation involving a shady art dealer and a disgraced movie producer. The case had ended successfully with the ring busted and the producer behind bars.

Now, her private driver whisked her to Beverly Hills to a swanky hotel equidistant from Rodeo Drive and the Sunset Strip.

Pauling checked in and brought her own single piece of luggage to her room on the top floor of the hotel. It was a decadent suite with a separate sitting area, television and private balcony overlooking the hotel's shimmering, turquoise blue swimming pool. Already there were multiple tanned bodies, all of them thin, laying in formation around the cool water.

At the last minute, Pauling had remembered to throw a bikini into her suitcase, although at the time she had figured she wouldn't need it. Now, she was glad she did. It there was time, she fully intended to go poolside and order something cold, fruity and alcoholic.

Pauling spotted the large welcome basket and stack of items on the desk to the right of the sitting area.

For now, she rolled her bag into the bedroom and unpacked by hanging the clothes that hopefully hadn't been wrinkled and placing the rest of it in the chic white dresser across from the foot of the bed. The bedroom also had its own balcony. Pauling left the sheer curtains closed.

Back in the living room she opened the gift basket and pulled out a chilled bottle of champagne. *How had they managed that*, she wondered? She assumed they had kept track of her itinerary and monitored if her flight had been on time.

There were some gourmet snack packs of fancy cheese and nuts. A thick bar of premium chocolate rounded out the offerings.

Next to the welcome basket was a note with the logo of Global Security Solutions. Henry Torcher had personally signed the note.

Pauling frowned. Torcher was already here and certainly staying at the same hotel. She studied a bead of sweat on the champagne. They must have known exactly when she was coming, as the ice in the champagne bucket was still fresh.

Beneath the note was a folder with tomorrow's itinerary. She scanned it quickly, noting the time of the keynote presentation – 11 a.m.

Pauling uncorked the wine and poured herself a glass, then walked out onto her private balcony.

On the pool deck, a man in a European swimsuit walked over from his lounge chair to a tented cabana in which sat several people. A hot tub sat at the other end of the pool deck, vacant.

Pauling turned and looked back into her room.

The suite was amazing. Very expensive.

She also wondered if it was wired.

Having spent the entirety of her nongovernment career in security, she knew the possibilities. Pauling went back into the bedroom, retrieved her purse and went into the bathroom.

She shut the door and studied the mirror, the sink, the shower head and the toilet itself.

Satisfied there was no surveillance in the small room, she dug out a gray electronic device the size of a pack of cigarettes. It looked like a portable battery charger because it was designed to do so. In fact, the word "charger" was molded onto the center of the device's body.

However, it was a top-of-the-line scanner built to detect a variety of electronic signals, including transmission signals, unusual radio and channel frequencies as well as infrared and night vision. Pauling powered the device on and then casually walked into the bedroom. From there, she made her way into the separate sitting area.

The device was connected to her phone via an app. Pauling held the scanner in her left hand down by her side while she held her phone in her right, as if she was checking for messages.

The app presented a graphic representing the input from the device. At least six spikes in the graphic's interface told Pauling what she needed to know.

Her room was about as thoroughly bugged as a room could be.

Torcher, she thought.

CHAPTER 21

TALLON ENTERED the Landmark Hotel and walked straight through the lobby. He glanced toward the front desk and saw no one checking in. A couple with a young child were waiting by the elevators, holding Disneyland paraphernalia.

Confident his watchers weren't inside, Tallon detoured from the elevators to the small restaurant located in the hotel. He spotted a maid's cart parked outside a laundry area and picked up a plastic tub that contained fresh hand towels.

He put it on his shoulders and walked through the restaurant where only one table was occupied. Tallon walked through the swinging doors at the rear of the space and entered the kitchen. To his right was a cook chopping vegetables, to his left, a dishwasher opening a cylindrical appliance from which steam billowed. Beyond, Tallon spotted an oversized double metal door and strode confidently through it.

Immediately, he was faced with a dumpster around which a privacy wall had been built. Tallon waited until the doors behind him were closed and then he tossed the plastic tub into the dumpster, scaled the wall and dropped on the other side.

Now, he was directly behind the hotel. A metal fence marked the border between the hotel and a retail store that appeared to be closed for the day. Tallon climbed the fence, cut through an alley and emerged one block over from the hotel. He walked down the street an extra block, then turned right. When he reappeared, he was a good block and a half north of the Landmark.

He paused and got his bearings. Across from his hotel was a small apartment building probably built in the fifties. There was a diner, a shoe store and a pawn shop. A used car lot was a little farther down, with a half-inflated Statue of Liberty fluttering in the breeze.

A bit beyond was an old-school casino.

Tallon debated. Ultimately, he went with his instincts and took up a position just past the apartment building. He used a food stand that was closed for the day to shield him from view. His watchers certainly would not have booked a room in the Landmark. They would have wanted to be able to keep him under tabs twenty-four hours a day.

The apartment building was perfect.

He also figured the surveillance team would work in shifts. Now that they thought he was back in his room, one would no doubt return to the apartment. Possibly just take a break or maybe to touch base with whomever was actually running the operation.

Tallon didn't care which one of his watchers returned to the apartment. No matter if it was the man or the woman, he planned to make their acquaintance.

For now, all he could do was wait.

Ultimately, he only had to wait an hour.

It was the man.

He walked up the street and Tallon saw him in the cantilevered reflection of the pawn shop's window. Tallon waited until the man had entered the apartment building and then he followed him inside.

It was dim and there was a lingering sense of mildew but Tallon caught sight of the man walking toward the elevator. Careful not to make any sound, Tallon trotted forward silently, reaching the man just as the elevator door opened. Clearly, this wasn't the A-team. The man had let his guard down believing the target was back in his hotel room. He considered himself off duty. Tallon was happy he was so unprofessional. True professionals engaging in surveillance of a man like Tallon would certainly know they were never off duty.

Tallon used his momentum to launch a running punch that crashed into the man's head just above his left ear. Tallon heard bone crunch and he crashed into the man, praying the elevator was empty.

It was.

A key fell to the floor and Tallon scooped it up and shoved the unconscious man into the elevator. The key had a tiny piece of white paper scotch taped to its fob. 4C it read.

Tallon punched the button marked 4 on the elevator and kept the man standing semi-straight. The elevator door opened and he dragged the man to 4C, unlocked it and dragged him inside.

It was totally empty save for a suitcase, a shaving kit and a hard-shelled case Tallon immediately knew contained weapons. He dropped the man unceremoniously onto the floor and searched the luggage but found nothing.

He opened the case. Inside were three handguns of various calibers with multiple sound suppressors. Tallon figured he had most likely just found the man who had killed Paco.

Henry Torcher's biography was next. He'd been born in Germany, educated in London, emigrated to America over a decade ago. His academic record was peerless as was his performance, which saw him climb the rankings of every company where he'd been employed. He also had at one point been a competitive bodybuilder and mixed martial artist. There was a gap in his official record from his first foray into employment and his eventual position at Global Security Solutions. The researcher couldn't find where he'd gone or what he'd been doing.

The rest of the documents provided more details but no breakthroughs. If Zeta Corporation was hiding something, so far they'd done a very thorough job of covering their tracks.

By the time Pauling finished the analysis, she'd lost most of the afternoon. So she showered, changed into a business casual outfit, and called her private car to whisk her to the convention – taking place in a modern, high-tech space that also featured as a contemporary art gallery and event space.

Pauling walked into the main entrance which consisted of towering tubes of white steel across which were strung silver cables. It felt like walking through a modern, high-tech highway overpass. She entered the main space. The floor was pickled hard-wood, the walls were white and adorned with oversized modern artwork. Various sculptures were placed in the corners of the room. Most of them were made of metal and represented abstract versions of human figures.

A small orchestra played classical music and a small army of servers carried trays of appetizers and drinks. Pauling was offered a glass of champagne which she accepted.

Eventually, she spotted Karl Furlong talking to an Asian man dressed in a brilliantly colored blue suit and wearing eyeglasses with white frames.

"Ah, Lauren," Furlong said. He gave Pauling a peck on the cheek and introduced her.

"Lauren Pauling, meet Charles Tse. Charles is Chairman and CEO of FlyWire, which I assume you've heard of."

"Of course," she said. "Nice to meet you."

FlyWire was one of the biggest and hottest companies in Silicon Valley and had maintained that status for several years, a feat unto itself. If her memory served her correctly, FlyWire was a conglomerate of multiple highly successful starts that spanned the spectrum of digital, mobile and computer technologies. Tse was one of the wealthiest people in the world.

"I understand Karl acquired your company recently," Tse said.

Pauling was surprised. Compared to FlyWire, her company had been tiny.

"Yes, it's in very good hands," she said.

"So are you retired or do you have a new company?" Tse asked, making a vague gesture toward the conference. In essence, asking her, *why are you here?*

"Lauren is still a part of our organization and I invited her here to learn about some of our newest clients. Her insight is invaluable."

"Yes it is," a voice said behind her.

Pauling turned and came face-to-face with Henry Torcher. He shook Pauling's hand but not Furlong's or Tse's. He must have been chatting with them previously, which made Pauling wonder if that's how Tse had known about her.

"Hello Henry," she said.

"Lauren, I'm so glad you could make it. I trust your travel and hotel have been acceptable?"

He gave her that same smile that was as cold as the ice bucket had been back in her room.

"Of course. Thank you."

The four of them made small talk until the room began funneling into the auditorium at the back of the room. Pauling excused herself, went to the restroom and checked her phone.

For some reason, she was worried about Tallon.

CHAPTER 23

LEAVING the dead man in the room but pocketing the man's weapon, ammunition and cell phone, Tallon slipped out of the apartment building and walked back to his hotel.

He didn't see the woman in the cream-colored pantsuit but he knew she was somewhere close by, watching.

Tallon took the elevator to each floor, peeking down the hallway. It wasn't until the third floor that he spotted a couple of housekeeping carts. He walked toward them and spied a lanyard that matched the corporate colors of the hotel.

He walked past, saw the woman in one of the rooms spraying cleaner on a mirror and he reached out and lifted the lanyard with the keycard attached.

Tallon went back to the elevator and pushed the

button for the floor above his own room. The doors opened and he stepped out onto the plush carpet. It was a dark red color like a cabernet wine and the walls were covered with a silvery wallpaper. A chair made of recycled twig branches sat to the left.

He turned and walked down the hall, following the signs to the room he wanted.

It had been Paco's, according to the text messages he'd read on the now dead man's phone. Part of their mission had been to keep an eye on Tallon, but also on Room 719.

Tallon slid the pistol from the back of his jeans into his hand and held it by his side. He used the stolen keycard to open the door.

He stepped inside and listened.

There was no sound.

He shut the door silently behind him and walked further into the room. He looked around the corner to the bed and was glad it was empty. Either the room wasn't booked or its newest guest hadn't arrived yet. Judging by the size and exclusivity of the hotel, he guessed it would be the latter.

Tallon was glad it was empty. He had been worried he would find some tired business executive had decided to take a catnap. Tallon put the key and lanyard on the desk and studied the room.

This was where Paco had been staying and

where he might have been killed. He studied the carpet. It wasn't the same color as the hallway, and it was different than the carpet in Tallon's room. That, by itself, didn't necessarily mean anything.

He studied it more closely.

No signs of bloodstains. In fact, there weren't any stains at all. He knelt down and smelled the carpet. It didn't have an odor like the obnoxious cleaners hotels use to disguise smell. It smelled like a carpet store.

Because it was brand-new.

Tallon was now convinced Paco was dead and that he'd been killed right here.

But why?

He didn't know.

Quickly, but thoroughly, Tallon searched the room. He found nothing.

His eyes fell on the small in-room refrigerator tucked discreetly inside a cabinet underneath the television. Tallon smiled.

During a raid in Mexico, Tallon and Paco had been tasked with finding the kingpin's secret stash of bank codes. They'd searched everywhere and in desperation, had torn apart the mini-fridge in the kingpin's home office. There, taped to the wiring on the fridge's back, was a file containing the codes.

From then on, Tallon and Paco had made jokes about whenever they were looking for something;

drugs, stolen guns, contraband, they always said: don't forget to look in the fridge.

Now, Tallon pulled the little unit out of the cabinet and heard the mini bottles of wine and beer crash around inside. He would have to hurry as he was making a lot of noise.

He ripped the fridge out and it tumbled forward, exposing its back.

At first, Tallon saw nothing. He grabbed a handful of cables and popped them loose. The action caused the refrigerator's rear plate to separate. Tallon knew it had done so not because of the force involved, but because someone had loosened the screws keeping the sheet of metal secured.

He pulled the metal further apart and glanced inside.

There, taped to the inside of the thin metal was an object.

A memory stick.

CHAPTER 24

"THERE IS A THREAT TO HUMANITY," Charles Tse told the packed auditorium. Behind him on a white screen was the FlyWire logo.

"Some of you may think it's a global warming. Others, fundamentalist terrorism. Or overpopulation. Global hunger. Disease."

Tse paced the stage in his electric blue suit. The overhead lights imbued him with an energy and the reflection off of his white eyeglasses captivated the audience. The room was eerily silent and no one was looking at their phones. Charles Tse was in complete command.

"While I don't deny that these are all real issues. If any of these thoughts popped into your head, I may even be inclined to agree with you." He held out his hand as if he was ordering someone to stop. "But only to a point."

He put his hand down and resumed his pacing. "I believe there is something much more dangerous at work in the world today, something so nefarious that it may signal the end of civilization as we know it and doom our future generations to a hellish existence."

Tse paused for maximum effect.

"What is it that keeps me up at night? What is it that I fear may be the undoing of everything we and our ancestors fought for?"

He waited.

Finally, he spoke.

"Income inequality."

A buzz among the audience came to life as people leaned down to whisper to those seated next to them.

Tse held up his hands.

"Trust me, I know what you're thinking." He smiled as his teeth glowed under the lights. "What kind of joke is this, right? Here I am, talking to a room full of the one-percenters. Or more accurately, the quarter percenters."

The audience chuckled as one. Pauling thought it sounded like self-serving laughter. She was wondering exactly where Tse was going with this.

She knew he was a multi multibillionaire. For him to be talking about the income gap? Hell, he could give all of his money away for starters. That would put a good dent in the discrepancy.

"But hear me out," he continued. "The current situation is simply not sustainable. The rich are getting richer and the poor are getting poorer and I say that as a man worth many billions of dollars. But if you look back in history and examine points in human civilization when the disparity between the haves and the have nots grew to an extreme – what happened?"

A few people shouted answers but Tse ignored them.

"Conflict. You had conflict. The kind that does irrevocable harm to our society and changes the world forever."

Pauling was intrigued. She happened to agree with Tse. In terms of personal wealth she was nowhere near the same ballpark as the chairman of FlyWire, but she'd done okay for herself.

The fact was, she probably qualified as a one-percenter.

However, she was intrigued to hear if Tse had any solutions because so far, at least in the U.S., varying degrees of discussion were taking place in DC, but as usual, politics meant each side had its own solution and no interest in working out a compromise.

"Politicians can solve this problem, but they won't," Tse told the audience. "So where does that leave us?"

The room was silent now, everyone waiting for the solution from the man many believed was one of the smartest in the world.

"We have to be the leading edge of the sword," he said. "We cannot wait for governments to hammer out a compromise because we all know they won't. While I am advocating for change, I am not advocating for working outside of the system. Because it simply can't be done. We have to voluntarily seek taxes on the wealthy. It is the only way."

A negative ripple made its way through the crowd.

Pauling had to smile. Verbalizing the T-word in a room full of mega millionaires was pretty damn gutsy, she had to admit.

"Taxation on the rich and wealth redistribution is the only solution," Tse said. "Instead of paying lobbyists to restrict taxation, we should do the opposite. We should hire lobbyists to push for legislation that taxes the wealthiest among us. We should also back candidates and governments who are willing to take on the richest among us. We need serious, fundamental change in our society or our society simply won't survive."

He stopped pacing and stood front and center. He looked somewhere above the center of the audience.

"The sharing of wealth. We can either figure out how to do it now, peacefully. Or we can wait and watch it happen violently. Where everyone will be victims, not just us."

He gave a slight bow and walked off the stage to less than thunderous applause.

Pauling wondered why everyone was so vigorous in their appreciation for the speech because the last time she checked, Tse hadn't offered a single concrete solution.

The man sitting next to Pauling leaned over and spoke softly to her.

"What'd you think?" he asked.

Pauling glanced at him. He had sandy brown hair, a T-shirt with the Kings of Leon logo, blue jeans and Chuck Taylor tennis shoes.

"I think he made some valid points. Realistic implementation of his theories? Not likely."

He gave her a tired smile.

"What do you think?" she asked.

"I think there's a lot more to the story," he said.

Pauling heard what he said but she was

distracted by the tattoo on his hand that ran the length of his arm.

It was rather elaborate depicting the body of a snake.

And on his hand, the head.

With oversized, hinged fangs.

A viper, Pauling thought.

CHAPTER 25

TALLON TOOK the stairwell back down to his floor, unlocked his room and went inside. He inserted the memory stick into his laptop and double-clicked the files.

The first file, labeled "Mikael Gladhus" showed an image of a man of vaguely European bearing wearing a suit and carrying both a briefcase and a laptop bag. Two more images were close-ups of the briefcase and laptop bag. The last image showed Gladhus at his desk, in a very impressive office, with the laptop open before him.

The next image showed a blonde woman.

Tallon studied the image.

"Holy shit," he said.

He clicked so the image filled his screen.

"Hello Sonia," Tallon said.

There was a knock on his hotel room door and Tallon quickly shut the laptop. He stood to the side of the door with the gun by his side.

"Vegas PD," a voice said. The voice was male.

Not the other watcher.

Tallon knew better than to use the peephole which was an easy way to take a kill shot in the eye.

Instead, he said, "What's your badge number?"

"1, 2, F U," the voice responded.

The tinny voice of a dispatcher matched with the creak of gun belt leather made Tallon confident they were the real deal. Plus, the attitude sounded just like a cop.

A visit from the local cops made perfect sense to him and he knew exactly how they'd found him so fast.

Dale.

Tallon cracked the door, standing sideways and using the internal metal tab, instead of a door chain, to guard against someone trying to throw open the door.

He saw two cops. They were both men and he knew right away they were the real deal, not impostors sent to finish the job that had been started with Paco.

There was no sign of the woman watcher.

Tallon didn't move to open the door all the way.

"How can I help you officers?"

"Can we come in or do you want to step out?" the first one asked. He was a heavyset black man with a tired expression on his face.

"Hold on," Tallon said. He ducked back into the room, set the gun on the bed, and grabbed his key card.

He then went out into the hallway and shut the door behind them.

"Okay," he said.

They held up a photograph of Paco. His military picture.

"Know him?"

"Sure do," Tallon said. "He and I were in the military together. He said he was going to be here in Vegas around the same time I was. We planned to meet up but he hasn't answered my calls. Why?"

The other cop, young white guy with a crewcut answered. "He's dead. Hikers found him in a canyon north of the city.'"

"Shit," Tallon said. "How?"

"Not sure. May have been foul play," the black cop said. "Any reason you were down at the coffee shop asking around, showing pictures of him?"

"Yeah!" Tallon said, trying to play the part of a former military guy looking for a good time. "He's a good dude. We were going to party down, man. He recommended this hotel, so I figured he might have already been here."

"What's your name? And you have an ID?"

Tallon gave them his information.

"So what happened, anyway?" Tallon asked. "I heard there was some kind of weird scene down by that coffee place. And then some big shot Silicon Valley guy got murdered? What's that all about?"

The black cop handed Tallon back his ID.

"Couldn't tell you, sir. Above our pay grade."

"A detective may follow up with some questions," his white partner said. "You going to be around for awhile?"

"Probably another day or two, unless the casino takes my money sooner." He offered a hearty chuckle but the cops simply glowered at him before walking away.

Tallon went back into his room and started packing his bag. He couldn't leave right away as he had to let the cops leave the area. It hadn't really surprised him that Paco was dead. It pissed him off, for sure. He was mostly glad that he'd killed at least one of the people responsible. Maybe he'd find out more.

Because he had a good lead.

If the blonde was involved in Paco's death, that was good news for Tallon.

Because he knew her. *Sonia.* A relatively low-level hitman with a shady past.

Even better, Tallon knew her boss.

He intended to have a word or two with him.

And get some answers.

CHAPTER 26

PAULING WAS SEATED NEXT to Karl Furlong for dinner. Across from them at the table was Charles Tse, along with a beautiful slender Asian woman he introduced simply as Hazel. To Furlong's right was Henry Torcher and seated next to Torcher was a woman with long brown hair tinted with highlights. She had slate-gray eyes and a classically beautiful profile. She looked like a supermodel, Pauling thought.

Torcher had briefly introduced her as Goda Becher, CEO of Zeta Corporation. Pauling was surprised to finally meet her. It also caught her off guard how strikingly beautiful she was. It was Pauling's goal to have a conversation with her. Unfortunately, she sat on the other side of Torcher and spent nearly all of the dinner in conversation with Tse's date, Hazel.

With clockwork efficiency, servers delivered plates with petite filet mignon, roasted truffles and baby asparagus. The food was impeccably prepared and delicious.

Pauling spent most of the meal discussing with Furlong his future plans for the business, as well as a long conversation with the man to Pauling's left, a real estate magnate and angel investor who was worth a very large fortune, thanks in no small part to his investment in FlyWire.

After dessert, a small dish of crème brulee which was yet another example of gourmet cuisine minceur which Pauling thought was mostly a way to drive up profit margins in a restaurant, Tse came around the table and sat in the empty chair next to Pauling. The real estate investor had momentarily left the table.

"I have a request," Tse said to Pauling and Furlong. "I would like the both of you to return to San Francisco with me. I have a new project I'm very excited about and since it both involves and requires the ultimate in corporate security, I'd love to get your take on things. Perhaps there are opportunities we can explore together. Your travel and accommodations will be taken care of, naturally."

Pauling thought about it. She knew Tallon was in

Vegas and her sister wanted her to come closer to the holidays. There was no need for her to rush back to New York.

"Of course," Furlong said immediately. Pauling inwardly smiled. She would have done the same thing if she were still running her company. This had the potential to be an enormous windfall for the firm.

"Yes, I am available and would love to hear about your new project," Pauling said.

Tse smiled. Pauling knew he hadn't for one second doubted their acceptance of his invitation. Few people turned down a business invitation from Charles Tse. "My assistant will follow up with the details," he said.

Tse returned to his seat and Pauling noticed that both Torcher and Goda Becher had left the table as well. That disappointed her. Part of the reason for her trip was to learn more about Zeta and now the elusive CEO had once again disappeared.

"Don't worry, they'll be joining us in San Francisco," Furlong said. He had noted Pauling's glance toward the vacated seats of Torcher and Becher.

"Very good," Pauling said evenly. She was determined to pin down Goda Becher and see what the woman could tell her about Zeta.

Pauling declined coffee and made her way out of the building. A car was waiting for her and she gave the driver her hotel's address. Out of curiosity, Pauling pulled her phone from her purse and launched an app.

Upon finding out that her room was bugged, Pauling had installed a simple camera she always carried with her when she traveled. It was nothing more than a basic surveillance camera embedded in the end of a pen. She had placed the instrument next to a pad of paper on the bookshelf in the hotel room's living area, pointed toward the door.

Now, she activated the app and waited for it to connect to the camera. Once it loaded, she re-started the camera's feed and hit Play. The camera was motion-activated so there was only two and a half minutes of footage.

It began when two men entered her room.

They were dressed in dark suits and made no efforts to conceal their identity.

Pauling had never seen the first man.

But the second one was her dentist friend from the flight out to Los Angeles.

Pauling had to admire whoever had planned this. They had a fairly good budget to afford this kind of manpower. Plus, the obvious conclusion was that whoever had booked her first class ticket from New York to LA had probably booked the phony dentist's as well.

Henry Torcher? she wondered.

She watched as they did a quick but thorough search of her room. One of them opened her laptop and tried a variety of passwords but she knew it was so thoroughly encrypted he would not succeed.

And he didn't.

They then carefully went around the room and removed the bugs they had planted. Which told Pauling they most likely knew she was checking out tomorrow. Or that they had already learned what they needed.

Finally, the men left the room.

Pauling smiled.

For the first time since she'd sold her company, she felt like she was back in the game.

CHAPTER 27

SONIA.

Tallon remembered her well. Two years ago on a mission she'd been the bait to lure an African drug lord out of his jungle compound.

The pre-mission briefing on Sonia had been clear; she was a woman willing to do anything and everything if the price was right. Good with a gun or knife. Equally adept with her hands, body and mouth. Not a top-tier assassin by any means, but a key player who could fill an important role in a mission like the one Tallon remembered. Tallon had never worked with her before but as he recalled, the mission had been successful.

Sonia had met the target at a brothel and distracted him while other members of the team had killed the drug lord's security detail. They'd ended up taking the drug lord alive, which had been the goal. If Tallon remembered correctly, he'd been debriefed and then turned over to his enemies.

They, certainly, didn't let him continue to breathe air for long.

People like Sonia, and to a lesser degree, Tallon himself, usually employed a go-between. Someone who could handle the necessary communication without fear of compromise. Sometimes it was a former member of the military who'd used the G.I. Bill to go to school for law and now had a thriving private practice. Lawyers were great to deal with contracts, which is what all private soldiers called their missions.

Tallon mostly worked with a former Special Ops communications specialist. He was an Ivy League graduate – University of Pennsylvania – who'd gone on to attend Wharton School of Business. He'd formed his own company and regularly farmed out work to people like Tallon. He was smart, loyal and one hundred percent above board.

The same couldn't be said of Sonia's go-between.

His name was DeGroot and there had been no Ivy League school in his background. Not much schooling at all, in fact, other than the streets. He was a bare knuckle brawler turned mercenary who was usually hired for missions that required a fairly thorough bending of the rules.

The reason Sonia had no doubt been chosen for the operation involving Paco was partly because of DeGroot's location; he'd set up shop on the outskirts of Las Vegas via an outfitting store creatively called DeGroot's Outdoors.

Tallon had been there once before on a mission that had never panned out. If memory served him right, he'd gotten cold feet when it appeared DeGroot was making stuff up as he went along. That was the perfect approach to take if you wanted to get a lot of your people killed.

From the outside, DeGroot's Outdoors appeared to be the kind of place hikers, campers, fishermen and hunters could gear up for trips into the nearby mountains.

But DeGroot had a whole back section of the store sealed off with high security. There, several rooms contained very hard-to-find weaponry, as well as offices and conference rooms designed to host planning sessions for missions at home and abroad.

Tallon pulled up into the parking lot and noticed there wasn't a single vehicle in front of DeGroot's.

He parked and walked to the front door.

There were no posted hours of operation. Tallon shook his head. He'd figured the "store" was mostly a front and tax dodge. But that was just lazy and sloppy to not even put in the effort to make it appear as a realistic retail enterprise.

Tallon tried the front doors and found them locked.

He walked around to the back of the store where a heavy-duty fire door was stationed beneath a security camera. The door was painted jet black. There was a button, large and red circled by polished steel next to the door.

Tallon pushed the button and waited.

Nothing happened.

He grasped the steel handles of the door and twisted them.

The door opened.

Tallon glanced to his left and then his right. No one appeared. He heard no alarm ringing so he stepped inside.

The place was pitch-black.

Tallon shut the door behind him. He pulled out a pocket flashlight, held it in one hand, and withdrew the gun from his waistband. There was no sound in the space other than the quiet whir from an overhead air-conditioning vent.

The space was a wide, empty opening most likely designed to receive shipments. To the left and right were matching wire shelving units containing boxes and plastic crates. The word *ammunition* was stenciled on several of the containers.

Ahead, a short hallway led to an office.

Tallon walked forward, aware that surprising a mercenary in his place of business was a very bad idea. The unlocked door, however, made him suspicious that he wasn't in any great danger.

DeGroot was either gone, or something worse.

It turned out, worse.

Tallon opened the door to the lone office and saw the body hanging from an exposed beam. The corpse was naked and clearly had been subjected to torture. Tallon spotted stab marks, slashing wounds and burns.

Paco.

Sonia.

DeGroot.

As well as Mikael Gladhus.

Tallon wondered if the watchers back at his hotel had been responsible. If so, he really didn't feel bad about executing the man in the apartment.

Maybe the woman in the cream-colored suit was looking for him.

Tallon hoped she would find him.

He was by no means finished with them.

CHAPTER 28

THE MAN KNOWN as Viper knew that his tattoo had not gone unnoticed by Lauren Pauling.

Now, he thought about the woman he'd sat next to during the monumental display of bullshit presented by Charles Tse.

Viper hadn't believed a word of what the con man said. He, with this flashy blue suit and stupid white eyeglasses, was all about himself. And money. But he was also an expert in marketing and public relations. Tse instinctively understood the power of a brand and how important it was to frame everything in that context. Steve Jobs had done it with Apple, and now, Charles Tse was doing it with FlyWire. But Viper knew that Tse had much bigger plans than just his current company. It was nothing more than a stepping stone – never mind the fact that it was a multibillion dollar stepping stone. No, Tse's greed went well beyond that.

Never mind that he, Viper, worked for Charles Tse. That was beside the point.

No, what mattered was reading between the lines and as a guy who had proven to be a virtuoso writing code when most of his classmates were worried about their complexion, Viper knew all about seeing beyond the obvious.

Like now.

Things hadn't worked out the way he'd wanted. He really thought things would have gone better and he thought he'd hired the right people to do the work for him.

It wasn't that he didn't want to get involved, it was just that he was meant to be a guy working a keyboard, not a gun. He wouldn't know the difference between a Glock and a water pistol.

Which is why he'd reached out for help.

Now, he needed even more help, unfortunately.

Viper pivoted in his chair and pulled the keyboard closer to him. He was in the "Viper Cave" as he liked to call it: a highly secure location designed to cloak all of his activities in secrecy. It was how he had discovered the information that had started this whole mess.

Viper was the only one outside the people

involved who knew what the big picture was. He didn't know all of it, but he thought he knew enough.

With a few keystrokes he effortlessly gained access to the cell phones of both Michael Tallon and Lauren Pauling.

They didn't know it yet, but they were both after the same thing.

It was his job to bring them together and do what others had failed to accomplish.

His pale, slender fingers blurred effortlessly as he tapped out a message.

He read it over, made a slight change in the wording, and then leaned back in his chair.

The screen lit up his face and he closed his eyes. He wanted nothing more than to be wrong. Totally and completely wrong.

But he knew he wasn't.

He reached out and with a single tap, sent the messages.

CHAPTER 29

TALLON WAS IN HIS SUV, heading directly away from DeGroot's Outdoors as fast as he could go without arousing suspicion.

His cell phone buzzed and he glanced at the screen.

An unknown number.

He also saw Pauling's name mentioned in the body of the message.

Tallon exited from the freeway and pulled into the parking lot of a home improvement store. He put the vehicle in park and picked up his phone. He read the message.

Pauling and Tallon,
You don't know me, but I know who you are.

Tallon, I know what happened in Las Vegas to you, Sonia and DeGroot. I know you just found DeGroot's body – don't ask me how I know. Pauling, I know you are on your way to San Francisco to meet with Tse and others.

This is a warning to you.

They are going to try to kill you.

Tallon, you are not in immediate danger, but I highly suggest you come to San Francisco. It's where I am and it's where Pauling is. You can drive here in 8 hours from your current location. Yes, I'm tracking you via GPS.

I know the both of you are tempted to ignore me and be skeptical, but we can help each other. There is something of great importance I must discuss with you. It has to do with the murders of Paco Williams and Mikael Gladhus, as well as Zeta Corporation and Charles Tse. It's much too complicated to state in a message like this, so please trust me.

. . .

Tallon, once you are closer to San Francisco I will send both of you a message with an address where the three of us can meet.

Please hurry.

Viper

Tallon read the message and immediately called Pauling.

She picked up right away.

"Viper? Is this for real?" he said.

"I think I just sat next to him in a meeting. I saw his tattoo."

Tallon listened as she filled him in on her trip to Los Angeles, what she found in her room, and the speech given by Charles Tse.

"What'd this guy with the tattoo look like?" Tallon asked.

"Blond hair, scraggly goatee. He had on jeans and a black T-shirt, Chuck Taylors. I assumed he was a computer guy, maybe a programmer."

"Young? Old?"

"Probably in his mid-to-late thirties. Hard to tell. What's going on with you?"

He filled her in on some but not all of what he'd done in Las Vegas, especially leaving out how he'd shot a guy in an apartment building.

But he did mention that the friend he'd come out to help was in fact now in a morgue somewhere. And that his death wasn't the only one to which he'd been exposed. No sense in committing anything in writing, albeit via text, regarding crimes. He would share the details in person with her later.

"So what do you want to do?" she asked him.

"Well, I'm merging onto the freeway, headed to San Francisco. I think putting a little distance between myself and what's going on here is a good idea. Plus, I'm curious to hear what you think."

"I don't know what to think, to be honest," she answered. "Something is extremely shady with Zeta Corporation, I can tell you that. Torcher brought a woman to dinner who claimed to be the CEO, but I have my doubts. He's been reluctant to share any details about the firm from day one. And now this mysterious message. I think that perhaps two heads are better than one. I'm looking forward to seeing you."

"Yeah, me too. I'm glad I'm driving so we'll have everything we need. I assume you're traveling light?"

Meaning – no weapon.

"That's right."

"Okay, I should be able to make it there in seven hours. Six if I really push it."

"Be careful, Tallon."

"Stay safe," he said.

He hung up, found his way to the fast lane on the freeway and stomped on the accelerator.

CHAPTER 30

THE FLIGHT from LA to San Francisco was shorter than the time it took Pauling to get her boarding pass, go through security and board the plane. When she landed, another car was waiting for her. She climbed into the back seat, and tried to relax as the driver headed toward the city.

She'd been to San Francisco a few times and remembered the area well. It was one of her favorite cities, especially for walking. She loved the steep streets and sweeping vistas. Not to mention great food.

Pauling was looking forward to having Tallon here. Someone to bounce ideas off. To reconnect and find out exactly what was going on with him. Who was Paco and how was he involved in the murder of Mikael Gladhus?

On a more selfish level, she was just looking forward to seeing Tallon, period. She'd missed him since they'd last been together.

The driver accelerated past a U-Haul – the most dangerous vehicles on the road – and moved into the right lane. Pauling saw rows of red taillights ahead. There was always traffic out here.

"Rerouting," the driver said.

He exited the freeway and soon they were on a service road, parallel to the freeway. They passed rows of strip malls and tract housing. Another turn brought them onto a rural highway that she figured would circle them back to the freeway, well ahead of the traffic jam.

Ahead, there was an ancient overpass. It looked like it had been built maybe fifty years ago with weeds and a rusty guardrail–

The gunshots shattered the rear window of the car and Pauling felt shattered glass drain down around her. In front of her, the driver's head sprouted blood as a bullet struck. Tufts of hair lifted and blood sprayed onto the inside of the windshield. His body slumped forward over the steering wheel. The car careened sideways and accelerated until it scraped the right wall of the overpass. There was the sound of metal shrieking and Pauling smelled burning oil and rubber. The car came to a sliding, grinding halt, halfway inside the tunnel.

Goddamnit, Pauling thought. *Perfect place for an ambush.*

There was nowhere to run. Even if she did, they would mow her down in seconds flat.

Instead, she dove forward over the back seat as more shots rang out. She heard the bullets punch into the metal and bits of steel and glass pierced the skin on the back of her arms and neck.

Pauling landed on the front seat and reached over to the driver's door. She pulled the release handle and pushed the driver out of the car onto the pavement. His blood acted as a lubricant and he slid easily out of the car.

Pauling pulled the door shut just as bullets shattered the window and sideview mirror. She glanced into the rearview mirror and saw two men exiting a dark sedan.

One of them she recognized as the man posing as a dentist on her first flight out – the same one who'd ransacked her hotel room.

Pauling found the gas pedal and pushed it forward, wrenching the steering wheel to the left. They were hooked on something but the car's big engine screamed and she again heard the sound of twisting metal and suddenly the big car broke free.

Behind her, she saw the two men separate. One started running toward her. One was racing back to the car.

Perfect, she thought.

She slammed on the brakes, threw the car into reverse and gunned the big car backward, straight into the running man who'd stopped and was aiming. The car hit him in the midsection and flung him backward.

Pauling kept the car going and felt the car run over the man on the ground. She hit the brakes again and saw his body now in front of the car. She steered the car forward and ran over him again, aiming the tires for his head. Once she was past, she again stopped the car.

She flung the door open and ran to the man. He was dead. His neck was clearly broken. Pauling found the gun still clutched in his hand. She heard an engine revving behind her and dove to her left, out of the way of the attacker's vehicle.

She landed in the middle of the road as the second car crashed into the one she'd just vacated. She took careful aim and as the second gunman leapt from the car, she shot him in the head.

He landed face-first on the pavement.

Pauling got to her feet, felt blood running down the backs of her arms and her knees were bleeding.

She went to the second dead man, found his gun and spare ammunition and then inspected the cars. The attackers' car, even though it had just rammed into the one she'd been riding in, was in better shape. All of its windows were intact. Pauling could drive it and not attract attention.

She had no intention of waiting for the police to arrive, even though there were no signs of anyone around. The killers had picked the perfect spot to make their attempt.

Too bad it hadn't worked out for them.

Pauling got into the car and then had a second thought. She went back to the two dead men, retrieved their cell phones and got back into the car.

She threw the cell phones and the guns onto the passenger seat and drove away, under the overpass, back toward the city.

CHAPTER 31

TALLON MADE the drive in just under six and a half hours, stopping only for gas and coffee. By the time he was less than a half hour from the city, a message popped up:

Tallon,

Pauling is waiting for you at this location. Please go there and retrieve her. Once I see that you've found her, I'll send you more instructions on where we can meet. Please be careful, they already tried once to kill her. They'll try again.

Viper

. . .

Just like he'd done before, the minute he was done with reading the message he called Pauling.

"What happened?" he asked. "Are you okay?"

"Yeah," she said. "A little shaken up. It's been awhile since I've been through something like that."

He heard her take a sip of water. She briefly described what had happened, leaving out certain obvious conclusions. He was glad she was hydrating. Adrenaline can take a lot out of a person and nothing gets the blood pumping faster than being shot at. He certainly knew that firsthand.

"I've got your GPS coordinates and my navigation mapped me to you. I'll be there in fifteen minutes."

"Okay."

As he drove, he felt an incredible sense of relief that Pauling was okay. He loved her and the idea that someone had tried to take her out infuriated him. He also tried to reconcile what had happened to Pauling in the context of what had just happened in Vegas. Whatever was happening was unraveling fast. There was big money at stake for this level of violence to exist.

He had more questions than ever and he couldn't wait to talk to this Viper character. If he was, in fact, real.

Tallon stayed on the highway for five more

minutes before taking an exit that led to a cloverleaf anchored by a huge truck stop. The nav told him to follow the road east, into a commercial strip of warehouses and equipment lots encircled by razor wire.

At a mall that consisted of a dollar store and several empty storefronts, he pulled into the second entrance at the end.

There were only three cars in the parking lot. Two were in front of the dollar store. The third was just past the store, near an empty building that looked like it had once been a Mexican restaurant. The sign above the door was blank, but shaped in the form of a cactus.

He pulled up next to the dark sedan and saw Pauling behind the wheel.

She got out of the car and he climbed down to meet her.

They embraced and he could feel her body in his hands, feel how tense she was. He felt the dried blood on her arms and looked her over.

"Later," she said. "Let's get out of here."

She went to the car and pulled out two guns and two cell phones and together they climbed into Tallon's SUV.

Once inside, he leaned over and kissed her.

He pulled out of the parking lot and drove slowly with no destination in mind. As he drove she told him the finer details of the ambush and how she'd made her escape.

"They underestimated you," he said.

"Last time for everything," she responded. "Okay, your turn."

Tallon gave a recounting of his moves in Vegas, including how he'd executed the watcher. Pauling was especially interested in DeGroot and Sonia.

"How did they get involved?" she asked.

"I don't know," Tallon said. "Maybe Viper has some answers."

Pauling looked out the window and Tallon saw her reflection in the window. She was tired. He was about to suggest they find somewhere to hole up when both of their phones vibrated with a new message from Viper.

"Hold that thought," she said.

She looked down and read the address out loud.

"It's about two miles away."

They punched the address in Tallon's navigation system and soon they pulled into another commercial parking lot, this one with apparently mixed use tenants. On one side was a stone and masonry business. In the center, a long-term storage facility with freestanding units that ran back in three sets of columns. To the right, a trucking business that seemed to be down on its luck. Only four trucks were in the lot and they looked to be twenty years old and not well taken care of.

"My guess is we're going in there," Tallon said. He lifted his chin toward the gated entrance to the storage units. A message came through on their phones.

"It's a code for the gate," Pauling said.

Tallon pulled the SUV up to the gate and Pauling read him the code out loud. He punched in the numbers and the arm lifted. Tallon pulled the SUV through.

"It's on the right," Pauling said, reading from her phone.

He turned the SUV right and then another left.

"There at the end," Pauling said.

Tallon spotted it. A lone storage unit with the door open.

Light was spilling out onto the darkened pavement. There was no other sign of life.

He drove forward and as they pulled up to the open storage unit, they each had a gun in their hand. Tallon held his low, just beneath the opening of his window. He was ready to fire, depending on what was inside the storage space.

As the unit came into view Tallon saw several banks of computer equipment all alight with green buttons and dials. There was a massive network of cables and electrical lines. It looked like the entire space was filled with computer banks.

A single man stood in front of them.

He had on a T-shirt, blue jeans and sneakers.

"Viper," Pauling said.

CHAPTER 32

TALLON PARKED the SUV beyond the end of the row of storage units and shut it off. He walked back to where Pauling now stood with the blond man.

"What the hell kind of name is Viper?" Tallon asked.

The blond man held out his hand. "Yeah, I know. Super lame. But online hackers, most of whom have the maturity level of fourteen-year-old boys, love cheesy nicknames. My real name's Paul. Paul Collins."

They shook hands and he looked at Pauling.

"Are you okay?" he asked. "I intercepted some law enforcement communication about two dead men out in the middle of nowhere, sort of by the airport detour. I wondered if that was you."

"I'm fine," Pauling said, neither confirming nor denying the question.

"The real question is, what in the hell are we doing here?" Tallon asked. "And what exactly happened in Vegas?"

"I've got some answers for you," Collins said. "Unfortunately, I don't have all of the answers. Here, let's go inside."

Pauling and Tallon stepped into the storage unit and Collins hit a button. The door powered down and locked into place.

"Quite a place you have here," Pauling said. "Do you have your own power?"

"Yes and no," Collins explained. "I started with what this facility provided and then found a way to bypass the main junction and divert what they need. The rest I commandeered and found ways to boost it quite dramatically. It's my own server system so I can do my work free of interference," he said. "Obviously, I've had to install massive firewalls which a lot of this represents." He waved his hand behind them toward the rows of computers.

"And free of scrutiny?" Tallon asked. "You know, from the authorities?"

"No, the authorities are the least of my concerns," Collins said. "Even if they wanted to investigate me, and I've given them no reason to be interested, it would take them a long time and a lot of financial investment to do it. It would also require a technical expertise they simply don't have."

"So you're not avoiding law enforcement. Who *are* you hiding from?" Pauling asked.

Collins held up his pale, slender hands. "Let's back up a little bit," he said. "First, I'm a programmer. I actually work for FlyWire."

"You work for Charles Tse?" Pauling asked. "It doesn't sound like you're a fan of his from that first message you sent."

"He's brilliant but I also believe he's dangerous."

"He seems harmless," Pauling said. "Besides, I think his position on bridging the income gap is admirable."

"I'll get to that," Collins said. "Here, have a seat."

He had pulled out two folding chairs and gave his high-tech office chair, which was in front of two computer monitors and a keyboard, to Pauling.

"I've been working for Charles Tse for five years," Collins said. "It was the second gig I had after Stanford."

"What was the first?"

"An app for sharing video that doubled as a dating service. I made a ton of money but it wasn't why I went to school. So when Tse offered me the job, I took it." Collins' face lit up and he seemed energized by the memory. "We revolutionized a lot of the way businesses work and invented new security measures to protect not just businesses, but people, too."

He paused and Tallon knew he was about to get to the point.

"About sixteen months ago I came across a top secret memo. And when I say top secret, I mean, really, really classified. As in it was written by Charles and intended for only five other people. In the world."

He paused again.

"Who were the other five?" Pauling asked.

"The most important, and wealthiest, CEOs of technology companies in the world."

"Let me guess," Tallon said. "Mikael Gladhus was one of them."

"Yes," Collins confirmed. "Now, it was really none of my business, but something in the memo caught my eye. It was written in a way that said almost nothing at all. It was like a puzzle to me. It was a fairly straightforward message that was as banal as anything could be."

"But it really wasn't," Pauling offered.

"No. Now, I love puzzles. So I ran every test imaginable and finally cracked the code. And I discovered that Charles was planning a series of business ventures with all five of these people. Four were men and one was a woman."

"So, what's the big deal?" Tallon asked. "These guys form deals all the time."

"Right, that's what I thought."

Pauling smiled. "That's why it caught your attention. If it was a typical deal, nothing shady, then why the subterfuge?"

"That's right. So I kept monitoring the system for more messages and there were a couple more but nothing specific that I could grasp. And then one stood out. It was from Gladhus. It wasn't in code. He said he was backing out of the deal. And it sounded like he had something he was going to use to torpedo the deal. For everyone."

Collins took a deep breath. "Then Charles sent a hurried message, not coded to a separate security unit. He ordered them to set up a meeting with Gladhus and retrieve his computer and any documents he had with him."

"You knew it was a hit, didn't you?"

Collins nodded. "I kind of figured they weren't going to treat him with kid gloves. Did I know that my boss, the famous Charles Tse, was going to sanction murder? No. But I was also in a delicate situation because I didn't really have anything I could take to law enforcement."

An idea popped into Tallon's head and he instantly knew it was right.

"Oh no," he said.

Collins nodded.

"Yes indeed."

"What?" Pauling asked.

Collins shook his head and answered with a voice tinged with both sadness and regret.

"I hired Paco."

CHAPTER 33

"YOU HIRED PACO," Tallon repeated. "How? And why?"

Collins smiled again. "Not to sound cocky but I'm pretty good at what I do. It was easy to find private security for dangerous jobs. There are message boards and Reddit discussions where you can find what you're looking for. Word was Paco Williams was one of the best."

"He was," Tallon said, bitterness in his voice.

"How did you hire him, though? Just call him up?" Pauling asked.

Collins shook his head. "I just created a fake business and sent it to Paco's unofficial manager. I guess that's what you would call him. Along with a hefty budget."

"And what exactly were you trying to accomplish?" Pauling asked.

Tallon had already told her all about Paco and what had happened, so she was following the flow of Viper's story.

"One, I wanted to send someone to protect Gladhus," Collins explained. "I thought about contacting him myself, but how would that have worked? Email? Messaging? He would have totally been suspicious, especially if he'd found out I worked for Charles. So, I figured the best thing to do was to protect him, get him to a safe place and then I would go from there. To be honest, I didn't have a grand plan. I was kind of making it up as I went along."

He shrugged his shoulders and Tallon and Pauling exchanged a glance. It was Tallon who spoke first.

"I guess what I'm missing is why a business deal would result in so much violence. I mean, drug dealers? Sure. The Mafia? Of course. But a group of technology gurus who own half of Silicon Valley? Since when are they employing hitmen and killing innocent people? What kind of deal were they putting together?"

"That's just it, I don't have a clear answer for you," Collins said.

"Well you must have some kind of vague idea,"

Pauling pointed out. "At least tell us your hunches. Maybe we can unravel it together."

Collins nodded. "Okay. Well, I can start with Charles himself. He portrays himself as this evangelical-type person." He leveled his gaze at Pauling. "Trust me. He's not. You've heard of the stereotypical Silicon Valley 'bro?'" He used air quotes to emphasize the word. "Well, Charles is one of them. Big time. He's a misogynist. He's greedy. And he's not above breaking the law. It just so happens he's a genius, too. And very powerful."

"So he's not who he claims to be," Tallon said. "Welcome to America."

"Right. But you asked me to tell you what my hunches are. Well, first, I don't think this business deal, whatever it is, is legal. I think it's probably a scam of some sort. But knowing how big Charles thinks, it's probably one of the biggest scams ever conceived. Like the kind that would have a global effect."

Tallon started pacing back and forth in the small space. The servers were still running, their green lights blinking on and off like high-tech Christmas lights.

"If they were going to rob someone, who would they rob? The markets? Banks?" Pauling asked.

Collins leaned forward in his steel folding chair

and clasped his hands together. "No, I don't think so. But I have one more hunch I want to tell you about."

"What's that?" Pauling asked.

"I don't think Charles Tse was the mastermind."

"Wait a minute, how could he not be?" Tallon pointed out. "You're the one who discovered his messages. It sounded like his plan."

"At first, I thought so. But do you know how I told you there were five people all together? Four men and one woman?"

Pauling and Tallon waited for Collins to continue. He took another deep breath.

"I recognized all of the men, but the woman was a bit of a mystery and at this point, I still don't know her name. I only know the name of her company."

This time, it was Pauling who made the leap.

"Zeta Corporation," she said. "Goda Becher."

A look of surprise crossed Collins' face.

"Yes," he said.

CHAPTER 34

"REMIND me again what Zeta Corporation is," Tallon said.

Pauling and Collins looked at each other. Collins lifted his chin toward Pauling indicating she should go first.

"I first heard of Zeta when my former company announced they'd landed a huge account – Zeta – but provided almost no information on them. I started asking around and soon was invited out here to learn more. But no information was provided."

"Shocker," Collins said, his voice thick with sarcasm.

"And then at the meeting where we met," she said to Collins, "I was introduced to Zeta's CEO, Goda Becher. But I never got a chance to talk to her."

"That's not her real name," Collins said.

"Check this out." He'd pulled the computer keyboard closer to him and tapped out a series of commands. Soon, an image of the woman Pauling had been told was Zeta's CEO filled the computer screen."

"Yep, that's her," Pauling said.

"It is indeed. But her name isn't Goda Becher. It's Astrid Verplank. She's a model, albeit not a supermodel by any means. She works mostly in Europe. Occasionally as an actress, too. Small parts mostly."

"So in this case, she was acting all right," Tallon said. "Hired to pretend to be Zeta's CEO."

"Which is why Torcher did such a thorough job of preventing me from speaking with her," Pauling said. "He knew I would have sniffed out a phony right away."

"If she isn't the CEO of Zeta Corporation, then who is?" Tallon asked.

"That's a great question," Collins said. "I don't have–"

A line of code filled his screen and behind them, the servers kicked into overdrive. The lights went from a steady flashing to a rapid pulsation, along with a beeping sound that seemed to Tallon like an emergency. He hoped it was only a test.

"Shit," Collins said. "They hacked into my

system. They know who I am." His voice had risen an octave and Tallon saw the fear on his face.

"We've got to get out of here," Tallon said.

"Charles just filed flight plans for Munich," Collins said, his fingers flying across the keyboard. "I set an alarm to track his movements. It's not a coincidence they broke into my network and suddenly, he's flying out of the country."

"Zeta is headquartered in Munich," Pauling said. "He's going to meet with her. The boss. Whoever she is."

"Seriously, we have to go–" Tallon started to say as he withdrew his pistol.

His voice was cut short by the sound of automatic gunfire. Bullets pierced the steel storage unit door. There must have been more than one gunman because the fire kept up at a steady pace. Through the holes in the door, Tallon could see the night sky.

Pauling and Tallon instinctively dove for cover.

Collins turned toward the entrance to the unit.

It was the last thing he did.

A series of bullets stitched across his chest and shredded his upper torso. He was knocked backward, flipped over his chair and landed on the concrete floor. Blood gushed from his wounds and seeped around his body.

"Follow me," Tallon said to Pauling. He was

belly crawling away from the door to the rear of the unit. There had to be an access panel. Somewhere for the cables and heat to go. Tallon noted there wasn't a ceiling vent. It had to be in the back.

More gunfire erupted from the front of the unit and Tallon heard an incredibly loud crash. They had driven a vehicle into the door. He glanced back and saw the door had been almost completely removed. Figures clad in black and armed with automatic weapons were charging inside.

They had to figure a way out.

Now.

He looked ahead and saw he was right. There was a vent at the rear of the unit. It consisted of an air-conditioning unit and compressor along with a thick collection of cable running through it. Next to it was a built-in fan whirring silently.

Tallon leaned back and kicked hard at the metal supporting the fan. It dented but hung in place.

"Stand back," Pauling said. Tallon ducked to the side and Pauling shot at the framework of the vent, focusing on the hinged corners. The thin metal, nothing more than aluminum, yielded easily to the bullets and holes appeared.

Tallon kicked again and the whole vent along with the fan, compressor and cables fell outside the back wall.

"Go," Tallon said. He turned and fired back at the figures now rapidly approaching them.

Pauling dove through the open square of metal and Tallon followed. He felt a jagged edge of torn aluminum rip open a gash in his thigh but he kept moving.

Pauling fired at something to her right and Tallon saw that a man dressed in black had appeared, ostensibly to cut off their escape. He fired off a round that went wide as Pauling's shot punched him in the chest. He dropped to the ground with his arms flung to the side.

Tallon scooped up the dead man's automatic rifle and tossed Pauling his keys.

"Let me keep them busy while you get the car," he said.

She took off into the darkness and Tallon stepped back. He brought the rifle to bear and aimed through the opening. He waited. When the light changed and he saw a shadow enter the space he let loose a stream of gunfire into the opening. He heard shouts of pain and cursing and then bullets were punching through the aluminum.

Tallon ran around to the front of the unit just as a figure emerged. Tallon fired a burst and the man was knocked backward.

Tallon pivoted around the opening, the rifle at his shoulder.

The men in back were now running forward to the opening. They were in single file.

Tallon mowed them down with a steady stream of rifle fire, keeping the muzzle down so his shots didn't go high.

And then, just like that, it was silent.

An engine revved and Pauling was behind him in the driver's seat of his SUV.

He dove into the passenger seat and they careened down the alleyway, crashed through the security gate and merged back onto the highway.

Tallon looked at his leg. His pants were soaked in blood.

"Are you shot?" Pauling asked, noticing his gaze.

"No. I'm fine." He looked out the window as Pauling steered the SUV onto the freeway.

"Where are we going?" he asked.

Her mouth formed a tight line.

"Munich."

CHAPTER 35

THE WOMAN STANDING before the floor-to-ceiling windows was well over six feet tall with broad shoulders and wide hips. She didn't stand straight, however. Instead, she leaned on a cane.

Munich, Germany, lay before her. The office in which she stood was on the top floor of a highly unusual, avant-garde structure hastily erected less than nine months ago.

It suited her. What was old was new again. Just like her.

Rebirth, in a sense.

Or reincarnation.

The old "her" was long gone.

That woman's name had been Gunnella Bohm. Head of the most secretive criminal organization in the world: the Zurich Collective. She'd helmed the group of the world's biggest and most powerful people for nearly a decade. Until she'd been blasted off the deck of a ship by an angry man with a shotgun.

He'd underestimated her will to live, however. She'd survived. For now, the woman had not exacted her revenge on the man who'd shot her. Patience was a virtue. She enjoyed savoring thoughts on revenge almost as much as she enjoyed exacting it.

No, for now, she was mostly concerned with regaining her wealth and power.

Which is why she'd escaped Zurich, set up shop in Munich, and assumed the identity of a woman who shared her initials: Goda Becher. It was also why she called her new outfit the Zeta Corporation. It wasn't a nod to her old firm but a message instead: she was going to replace the Collective with her new organization.

By starting things off with a bang heard 'round the world.

Which brought her mind around to Charles Tse. Her poor, incompetent Asian genius.

He was on his private plane to come and see her. To try to explain how he'd bungled things on his end.

It didn't matter.

She would make it all better.

Besides, he'd served his purpose. She had needed

him to engineer the cooperation of the other Silicon Valley executives. The cream of the one-percenter crop. Like-minded individuals who shared a similar goal: wealth. The more, the better.

At any cost.

As long as the cost was someone else's burden to bear.

The woman turned and walked back to her desk. It stood nearly four and a half feet tall so she could work standing up. It was her way of getting stronger. Plus, she liked pain. Especially in the bedroom with subservient lovers. She employed pain at every opportunity in both her personal and professional lives.

For the first time in a long while, she felt the old surge of excitement. It's the emotion one feels when making a big, bold strategic move that could have enormous payoffs, combined with the element of disaster. The tightrope between mind-boggling success and brain-numbing defeat.

With Charles Tse soon to be safe in her pocket, it was time to put the rest of the plan in place.

Her fingers tingled with excitement as she tapped out a message on her highly encrypted phone.

She hit send and knew that as soon as the message was delivered, the world would never be the same.

CHAPTER 36

WASHINGTON, DC

He watched as the long black limousine pulled up to the restaurant. It was an exclusive Italian eatery less than twenty minutes from the Capitol and a frequent choice for high-ranking government officials. *Washington's elite*, as they no doubt referred to themselves.

A woman dressed in a blue power suit stepped out of the limousine flanked by her security detail. She went inside the restaurant joined by one of her security team. The driver of the limo parked the big vehicle in a valet space and then stood outside the vehicle. He would remain there until the woman was through with her meal.

The man watching from the rooftop across the street knew what was going to unfold inside.

The congresswoman would be immediately seated at her favorite table. It was in the back corner of the restaurant.

She was legendary for power lunches and the man on the rooftop knew today would be no exception. He had been following the woman for more than two weeks and at this point, knew her schedule probably better than she did.

He had a high-powered sniper rifle at his feet. It was probably overkill for this kind of shot, but it was always better to have a little extra firepower than not enough. You never knew what could happen.

He'd rehearsed his movements and the minute she stepped out of the restaurant, she would be a dead woman.

The congresswoman in question was chairman of the House Ways and Means Committee, which made her a woman in high demand. Not just from her fellow politicians, but also lobbyists representing businesses who could potentially be severely impacted, in good ways and bad, by her decisions.

The man on the rooftop had his own suspicions about who'd hired him to kill the congresswoman. He was fairly certain his employers had been, or would be, negatively impacted by actions taken in the woman's duties.

It didn't matter to him.

He'd just received the message he'd been waiting for.

One word.

Go.

CHAPTER 37

LONDON

The woman in the rented flat waited for her lover. His last name was Graham and he was known far and wide as a champion of the people. In most circles, the moniker was uttered in sincerity. In others, it was said with wry amusement.

It didn't matter to her.

She supposed that a man who forcefully spoke of the need to stand up for the "little people" ought not be unfaithful to his wife. Yet, history was replete with iconic figures known for their lofty achievements who hadn't been above wrestling between the sheets with folks of the opposite gender and to whom they were not joined in holy matrimony.

The woman in the flat wore her usual; a provocative dress with high heels and a single strand of pearls. No panties.

Graham loved to twist the necklace in his hand when they were having rough sex. Another favorite activity of his that might register as a surprise among his loyal followers.

Tonight, however, her outfit included a new accessory.

A razor-sharp stiletto safely ensconced just below the line of her open-backed dress.

She intended to have a rousing bit of sex with Graham, one in which she would no longer be submissive but instead, punish him for her own pleasure.

And then she would perform the act for which she had been promised a very large sum of money.

She would slit her lover's throat.

CHAPTER 38

PARIS

The car was a vintage Porsche. Rare, but not overly so. Its owner, a Frenchman, drove it every evening down to his favorite eatery; a corner bistro with a dazzling wine list and crusty bread.

Now, the Porsche was in its preferred space in the garage. The man underneath the vehicle was not a mechanic.

He was a bomb maker.

At the moment, he was putting the finishing touches on the installation of one of his homemade devices. They were expensive to begin with. Even more so if they required the service of their creator.

But the bomb maker had been given an extraordinarily large sum of money as a deposit, so he had accepted the job.

He knew little about the Porsche's owner, other than the fact that he ran a popular website espousing views in favor of the lower class and sharply targeting the excesses of the rich.

Well, the bomb maker thought, perhaps when the Porsche's owner was blown skyward to Heaven, he would be able to rest easy knowing his killer was a working man.

No, the bomb maker thought. Probably not true. At that point, solace would be hard to come by, he guessed.

CHAPTER 39

MUNICH

Gunnella Bohm's back was hurting. She used the cane to cross her office, walk down the hall and enter a room with a single round white table that faced an oversized screen.

She powered the screen on and her assistant, a young woman with dark skin and almond-shaped eyes appeared in the doorway.

"Do you need my assistance?" she asked.

"Yes. Others are arriving soon. Have coffee, water and champagne ready."

The assistant left and Bohm gazed at the screen.

There were nearly a dozen small green lights on

the screen representing targets whose elimination she had just authorized.

When the green lights turned to red, it meant that particular objective had been neutralized.

It was going to be immense fun.

Not only would she be responsible for killing an American congresswoman, she would also rack up kills that included a member of British Parliament, a leader of the global liberal media and many more targets that collectively represented a powerful force for the poor in the world.

Gunnella Bohm thought it would be a crowning achievement in her career.

Afterward, she would enjoy a great deal of champagne, along with the slender assistant who'd just offered her assistance. She was new.

Brand-spanking new, so to speak. The pun made Bohm smile.

And Gunnella had yet to sample the assistant's obvious wares.

She licked her lips in anticipation.

CHAPTER 40

THERE WAS a Lufthansa flight direct from San Francisco to Munich. Pauling and Tallon were on it, thanks to Pauling's uber elite American Express. It was made of a weird color Tallon had never seen.

"He's got a pretty big head start on us," Pauling said.

They were seated in business class. She was exhausted. There'd been virtually no time to change her clothes or even take a shower.

"Yeah, there's that," Tallon said. He'd ordered himself a beer and was enjoying it very much, Pauling judged. "Why don't you get some sleep?" he asked her.

She took his advice and much later, she slowly came awake. Tallon was watching her. She smiled and asked, "Have you been awake this whole time?"

He shrugged. "Off and on."

They talked about Collins, what the authorities might have in store for them when they got back.

"It couldn't be helped," Tallon said of their decision to leave the crime scene and get a plane for Europe. "We'd be tied up in interrogations for days with our lawyers and the cops. Meanwhile, whatever is supposed to go down would be happening. We had to leave. Although I do feel bad about leaving Collins there."

Pauling agreed. "We have to find out what's going on. I've got a bad feeling about this."

They flew in silence until the plane landed and then they passed through customs and grabbed a rental car.

Tallon drove as Pauling went through her phone. "When I had my researcher look into Zeta, he gave me an address that supposedly belonged to Zeta. Who knows if it's real or not. Nothing's been real about them so far."

"So how'd he find it?"

"I thought it was better if I didn't know."

"You're probably right."

Tallon maneuvered his way through the airport and hopped onto the road heading south toward Munich. To the right of the entrance was a row of shops including, incongruously, a Victoria's Secret.

"Think more people buy lingerie when they arrive or depart?" he asked.

"Arrive."

Tallon considered asking her if she wanted to pop in and try on a few things but thought better of it. Instead, when they were still a good ways from the city center, Tallon pulled off the main road and drove to the east.

"Where exactly are we going?"

"A bar."

"This is no time for happy hour, Tallon."

"Trust me."

Which, of course, she did. They passed a sprawling army base that seemed to go on for miles.

"Joint base," Tallon explained. "Fair amount of American soldiers get stationed here usually for relatively short deployments."

They drove past the base to a beer garden that Tallon apparently knew quite well. They went inside.

"Hopefully the same guy works here," he said. When he asked a server for Wolfgang, he was met with a shake of a head.

Tallon explained what he was looking for and was referred to a bartender who'd been smoking a cigarette out back.

He waved Pauling and Tallon to a back corner of the bar where a door opened up into an office.

Using a mixture of broken English and German, Tallon said, "There was a guy who used to work here. He would buy certain items from soldiers leaving Germany to go back home. You used to be able to pick up a thing or two for cheap, without having to deal with paperwork."

The man nodded, then made obvious glances at Tallon's pockets and Pauling's purse.

Pauling pulled out a wad of cash and put it on the desk.

The man stood, opened a cabinet and Tallon saw a wide range of handguns. He chose two Berettas, both 9mm, and extra ammunition. He examined the guns and saw they were well-oiled with actions that were smooth.

They got back into the car and less than a half hour later, they pulled up outside the address Pauling's researcher said was the home of Zeta Corporation.

"Seriously? This is it?" Tallon asked. It was a strange-looking building. Contemporary, clearly, with sharp angles, and a minimalist exterior. Yet, it also seemed odd. Off-balance. As if it was either not finished or someone had borrowed surplus building materials and slapped the place together with whatever they could find. It was like a modern art piece that begged the question: is it *supposed* to look like this?

"Indeed it is," Pauling said.

"What's our plan?"

"Well, my guess is Charles Tse, Henry Torcher and the mysterious CEO of Zeta are all inside. I think we ought to introduce ourselves."

They got out of the vehicle with Berettas held loosely by their sides, and walked toward the building.

CHAPTER 41

"YOU CERTAINLY WENT OUT with a bang, as the Yanks like to say," Gunnella Bohm said.

She had her cane by her side. She was now joined in the room with the map monitor by Henry Torcher and Charles Tse.

Tse wore an emerald green suit and his glasses sported thick black frames. Torcher wore a black suit with a white shirt. His neck muscles were bulging and in his thick hand was a delicate glass of champagne.

"How are the rest of our colleagues doing?" Bohm asked.

"Mikael Gladhus is dead, of course," Tse said. He put a briefcase on the table. "This is what he had with him when he died. Copies of our exchanges and the plan in general. He was going to the authorities. That was a close call."

"Yes, I'm aware of that," Bohm remarked impatiently.

"The other two members of our consortium are alive and well and watching safely from afar," Torcher said. "One in his penthouse in Hong Kong. The other, on his cattle ranch in Argentina."

"Perfect," Bohm said. "What about the mess in Vegas?"

"Relatively under control," Torcher said cautiously. "Just a couple of loose ends. We found the leak and neutralized him."

"Good," Bohm said. "But explain what you mean by 'relatively.'"

Tse, standing by the side cabinet that held several magnums of champagne asked, "May I get you a drink?" he asked Bohm.

"Champagne," she responded.

Tse poured two glasses of champagne. Kept one for himself and handed the other to Bohm. His eyes went to the screen, willing the green dots to turn to red.

Which is why he was completely unaware of Torcher behind him. He'd set down his glass of champagne and now his enormous hands went around the Asian's throat and with a brutal twist, broke the man's neck.

The well-dressed billionaire slid to the floor, his glass of champagne spilled onto his suit. His glasses had fallen off and Torcher stomped on them. "I'm so goddamned sick of those glasses. I've wanted to do that for a long time," he said.

"Well done," Bohm said to Torcher. "It's good to see you again, son."

Torcher nodded. He hardly knew his mother but praise was almost never forthcoming.

He was about to respond when the map on the screen changed to a live video of the front entrance to the building.

They both watched as two people approached.

"Lauren Pauling," Torcher said.

"And Michael Tallon," Bohm responded. "This is what you meant by *relatively*?"

She turned and looked at her son.

"Please take care of them once and for all."

CHAPTER 42

TALLON RAISED his pistol and shot out the camera over the front entrance to Zeta Corp. He turned and spotted two more cameras, one on each end of the building. He took careful aim and shot them as well.

They shattered and the pieces sprinkled to the ground.

He motioned Pauling to go to the left and he took the right.

Inside, he could hear footsteps but also knew whoever was guarding the place was not going to come out of the front door.

There had to be a side entrance.

Sure enough, a door cracked open on the other side of the wall. Tallon waited. It was only one set of footsteps but the man was moving quickly. Not with enough caution.

Tallon raised the 9mm to eye level. When the man peeked around the corner, Tallon shot him. He had ducked back quickly and the bullet tore off his nose. Tallon dove around the corner and the man fired, the bullets going high. He was screaming in pain.

Tallon fired his gun five times in quick succession and the man stopped screaming.

Tallon crawled further around the corner so he couldn't be viewed from the front. He'd never seen the man before. Short, close-cropped black hair. Black pants and a heavy black sweatshirt with a vest. Security, for sure. Tallon wondered how big the security force was. There were no cars visible anywhere and no sign of life. If Zeta was in fact a fake company, how many people could they possibly have inside?

The rear of the building was the place to go.

They would try to flank them, for sure. Tallon raced forward, ducked around the back of the building and was surprised to see no one. He continued on, and turned the corner that should have brought him to Pauling.

But she wasn't there.

He turned, and came face to-face with a giant hulk of a man with blond hair and blue eyes.

His face was bright red and he was smiling at Tallon. His gun was pointed at Tallon's midsection and he started to say something.

Tallon didn't hesitate.

He drove his forehead directly into the man's face. Since the blond hulk was taller, Tallon's forehead only succeeded in smashing the man's mouth. Ordinarily, he could knock a man unconscious but the size difference had made it impossible. Still, Tallon both felt and heard all kinds of things breaking in the big man's face.

The man's gun erupted and Tallon felt something wicked strike him in the left side. It was a brutal blow and he knew he'd been shot. The strength began to seep from his body and he barely managed to stay on his feet.

And then two things happened almost instantaneously; he heard a single gunshot and his face was instantly covered with blood. His eyes were full of red and he couldn't see. The giant fell on top of him and Tallon crawled out from underneath the enormous body. He wiped his eyes with his bare hands.

He looked up and saw Pauling standing, her Beretta still pointed at the blond who was missing half of his head.

"Thanks," he said to her.

"You're shot, aren't you?"

"Afraid so," Tallon said. "Let's go"

CHAPTER 43

THEY ENTERED the building through the side entrance and were shocked by what they saw. It was completely empty, save for a lone elevator shaft in the middle of the space. It was all concrete, steel beams and exposed wiring.

No stairs at all.

No other signs of security.

"I don't like this," Pauling said, looking at the elevator. She was almost in disbelief. Zeta Corporation was a complete scam. The place was practically empty.

"Yeah, that's bad," Tallon said. He was wobbly and knew that climbing into an elevator and then having the doors open was the worst kind of exposure possible.

"There has to be stairs somewhere."

They went back to the front entrance.

"There," Pauling said. She'd spotted a concealed rectangle of space above which a crude fire escape ladder had been installed. Pauling ran to it, pulled the ladder down and they climbed. Pauling went up quickly. Tallon labored up, one step at a time.

At the top, an empty corridor led to a wall of glass.

They walked quickly, before noticing the two rooms at the other end of the hall.

Pauling stepped into the first, gun drawn and at the ready.

Tallon stepped into the second. It held a table, large flat-screen television and a shelf with buckets of champagne. Charles Tse was dead on the floor.

Tallon ignored the body and went out to the main space. He saw a woman with a cane and a small Asian woman running for the ladder.

Tallon fired but he knew his aim was off. The gun wasn't steady in his hands. Even so, the big woman stumbled, dropping a briefcase and laptop in the process. She pulled the Asian woman closer to her and used her as a shield.

His side soaked with blood and his balance questionable, he staggered forward and retrieved the briefcase as he heard Pauling run up behind him. He fell to the floor, sat up and opened the briefcase.

Pauling joined him and he held out the paper.

"What is this?" he asked. His face was ghostly white and blood covered his pants.

Pauling scanned the papers. "Jesus Christ. Charles Tse wasn't going to close the income gap," she said. "He was going to blow it wide open."

She showed the papers to Tallon.

"These are targets. People who wanted to tax the rich and redistribute wealth. They were going to assassinate all of them and make even more money."

"We have to stop them," Tallon said. "But how?"

Pauling spread the papers out and took photos of them with her phone.

"We won't," she said as she began firing off messages. "But the FBI and Interpol will."

CHAPTER 44

48 HOURS LATER

Tallon's hospital room was clean and the other bed was empty. He was recovering from surgery to remove fragments of a bullet lodged against his femur and hip.

More importantly, Pauling was sitting on the edge of the bed and they were both watching the television.

"A conspiracy to target various members of the global economy were thwarted today," the announcer said. "Authorities in America killed a man who planned to shoot the chairwoman of the Ways and Means Committee. In Paris, a member of Parliament was almost murdered by a woman with a knife. She was killed by police."

The reporter continued as a graphic showed a map with designated locations around the globe. "In other parts of Europe and all around the world, authorities were alerted to potential attacks. They were all stopped in time save for one, a car bomb in Paris that took the life of a prominent blogger who argued for vigorous measure to redistribute wealth in the world."

Pauling shook her head. "Greed. One of the worst cases I've ever seen."

The announcer continued. "The investigation is just beginning with reports of crimes committed in Los Angeles, San Francisco, Paris, London and Munich."

A nurse came in and checked on Tallon. Pauling shut off the television and remained silent until she left.

"The big woman with the cane," Pauling began. "The CEO of Zeta. You're telling me she had been the head of this group called The Zurich Collective?"

Tallon nodded. "Do you remember that case we worked where I introduced you to a guy who'd worked with me on some contracts? We talked about a loose collection of independent contracts that had been dubbed the Department of Murder? A group loosely affiliated with the Zurich Collective?"

"Yes," Pauling said.

"Well Gunnella Bohm was the head of the Zurich Collective for a long time. Ruthless. Someone murdered her, or so they thought. Rumor was the killer was an Italian businessman by the name of Marcus Benedetto. No one could prove it, though."

Pauling connected the dots.

"So let me guess, she came back and started a rival organization she called Zeta. I suppose she thought this insane plan with Charles Tse was going to put her back on top. Maybe her plan was to put her old company out of business. And get filthy rich in the process."

Tallon nodded.

"Yeah, that didn't work out so well for her, did it?"

CHAPTER 45

ZURICH, SWITZERLAND

The man who replaced Gunnella Bohm as head of the Zurich Collective still held the position.

His name was Dieter Mueller.

He was now standing in the office space reserved by the firm. They did not meet often as a group. Normally, those sessions were held at most twice a year. Sometimes, when everyone's business was thriving, only once a year.

As part of his compensation for assuming the mantle of one of the most powerful and secretive organizations in the world, Mueller had the use of the private apartment on the same floor as the offices.

It had once belonged to Gunnella Bohm. Once he'd taken over, Mueller had stripped the apartment down to its bones, hoping to rid the place of any remnants of Bohm.

It clearly hadn't worked.

Like Lauren Pauling and Michael Tallon, whose names he had been forced to become familiar with, he too had been watching the news. Thanks to their pipeline into Interpol and other law enforcement agencies, the firm had been able to see firsthand the evidence procured by investigators.

Not only were they monitoring the outcome and ramifications of the Silicon 5 as the media had dubbed them, but the Collective's interest was mainly with the only one of the group to have escaped.

A mysterious woman said to be in charge of a large firm known as Zeta Corporation.

Mueller now knew the truth. Zeta Corporation was a scam. A last-ditch effort by Gunnella Bohm - who most had believed was dead. Who no doubt at this point was certifiably insane.

Dieter weighed his options.

Finally, he deployed an order.

It was to the internal network of trained assassins known by its nickname: the Department of Murder.

He offered the largest single contract ever put into play by the Collective.

To realize the enormous payday, only one thing was required by Dieter Mueller.

Bring him the head of Gunnella Bohm.

BOOK #12 IN THE JACK REACHER
CASES

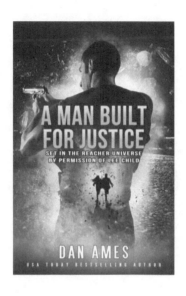

A USA TODAY BESTSELLING BOOK

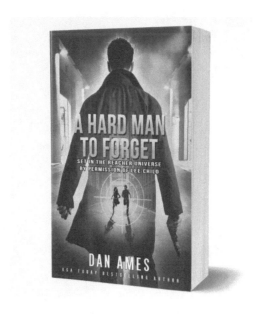

Book One in The JACK REACHER Cases

A FAST-PACED ACTION-PACKED
THRILLER SERIES

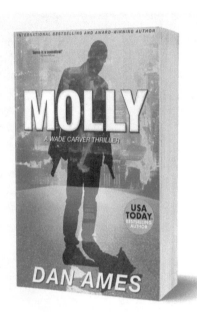

**Would you like a FREE copy
of my story BULLET RIVER and the
chance
to win a free Kindle?**

**Then sign up for the DAN AMES BOOK
CLUB:**

AUTHORDANAMES.COM